INDIAN COUNTRY

Finally Bill and Josh reached a fork in the trail. The right fork marked the beginning of the reservation. A sign in English declared this property off-limits to whites and instructed them to take the left fork.

"It could come any time now," Wild Bill told Josh as they bore right. "They've been watching us for a long time."

Josh was about to ask how Bill knew that. But almost the very moment they passed the warning sign, a series of yipping war cries made the hair on Josh's nape stand up.

At least a dozen well-armed, mounted braves suddenly descended from the tree cover and surrounded them. Josh stared at the angry, clay-covered Indians, his mouth dry with fright.

Bill, however, merely raised one arm high with the hand open—the universal sign for peace. He kept his face calm and impassive. Seeing him, Josh followed suit.

A warrior snatched the scattergun from his boot.

Other *Leisure* books by Judd Cole:

The *Wild Bill* series:
#1: DEAD MAN'S HAND
#2: THE KINKAID COUNTY WAR
#3: BLEEDING KANSAS
#4: YUMA BUSTOUT
#5: SANTA FE DEATH TRAP

The *Cheyenne* series:
#1: ARROW KEEPER
#2: DEATH CHANT
#3: RENEGADE JUSTICE
#4: VISION QUEST
#5: BLOOD ON THE PLAINS
#6: COMANCHE RAID
#7: COMANCHEROS
#8: WAR PARTY
#9: PATHFINDER
#10: BUFFALO HIDERS
#11: SPIRIT PATH
#12: MANKILLER
#13: WENDIGO MOUNTAIN
#14: DEATH CAMP
#15: RENEGADE NATION
#16: ORPHAN TRAIN
#17: VENGEANCE QUEST
#18: WARRIOR FURY
#19: BLOODY BONES CANYON
#20: RENEGADE SIEGE
#21: RIVER OF DEATH
#22: DESERT MANHUNT

WILD BILL
JUDD COLE

BLACK HILLS HELLHOLE

LEISURE BOOKS   NEW YORK CITY

A LEISURE BOOK®

September 2000

Published by

Dorchester Publishing Co., Inc.
276 Fifth Avenue
New York, NY 10001

ISBN 0-8439-4770-5

Printed in the United States of America.

BLACK HILLS HELLHOLE

Chapter One

"This is one of the hardest things I've ever done in my life," W. B. Hickok announced solemnly. "It's tough saying good-bye to an old friend like you."

Bill sighed, then squared his shoulders to do his unpleasant duty. "It can't be helped, damn it all. So long, old companion."

Whistling the sad German dirge "I Once Had A Comrade," Wild Bill bent closer to a polished-metal mirror nailed to the wall. In a series of fancy flourishes, he used an ivory-handled straight razor to scrape off his neat blond mustache.

New York Herald reporter Joshua Robinson stared at his famous companion, impressed by the striking transformation. Hickok had also just finished hacking off his long curls with a skinning knife. Most of the blond was in those curls, the hair not protected from sun-bleaching by Bill's hat. The hair he had left uncut formed a dark brown thatch.

"You look like a different man," Josh marveled.

"Give the lad from Philly a cigar," Bill replied. "That's the whole point of butchering my good looks. Kid, in the name of duty I just disappointed every red-blooded woman in America."

"But at least you've still got your modesty," Josh baited him.

"Modesty," Bill repeated in a curious tone. "Modesty, modesty . . . I know that word. French, ain't it?"

Josh laughed and gave up. No man was harder to rowel than Wild Bill Hickok.

The two of them shared a supply-train boxcar that had been made surprisingly comfortable for them and their horses. The sliding door was halfway open for ventilation and light. But the blast-furnace air gave little relief. These were the dog days of August in the Dakota mining country. To Josh, sweat-soaked from his hair to his socks, it felt more like Dante's First Circle of Hell.

"What kind of town is Deadwood?" Josh inquired.

"Town? Huh!" Wild Bill scoffed. "It's a bear pit. And all new arrivals are the bait."

Wild Bill's fear of being recognized in Deadwood, Josh realized, must be strong indeed. Not only had the frontier dandy sacrificed his hair and mustache—he had abandoned all vestiges of his usual sartorial elegance.

Gone were the silk vest and gold watch, the dark twill suit with a long duster to protect it. Now

Hickok was dressed "common as your Uncle Bill" in modest range clothes and a clean neckerchief—everything faded enough to suggest a working cowboy now turned saddle tramp. Even his custom-made Miles City boots had been replaced by clumsy work shoes with welt stitching.

"One thing I don't get," Josh said, thinking out loud. "Pinkerton says three of his operatives have been killed trying to infiltrate this vigilante gang. But how'd the bad guys know who and what they were?"

Bill cursed mildly when he nicked himself with the razor. "Kid, do you *have* to keep mentioning dead Pinkerton ops?"

Josh watched Bill dab a little calomel lotion on the cut. Hickok was not an edgy man by nature. But the mining town of Deadwood, South Dakota, held a special place in the pantheon of frontier hellholes. Hickok considered it infinitely tougher than even the cowtown of Abilene, Kansas, which Bill had once tamed as sheriff—though only briefly.

Besides all that, a prophecy made popular by Martha "Calamity Jane" Canary predicted that Hickok would someday meet his fate in that wide-open, untamed mining town. Bill wasn't superstitious. On the other hand, Deadwood was a damned likely place to die when your hide was worth $10,000 in gold.

"Speaking of mentioning things," Bill added, patting the shaving soap off his face, "you be damn careful what you write for that crapsheet of yours up East."

His eyes met Josh's in the mirror.

"This is an open case," Hickok added, "which means every dispatch gets cleared through me before you send it."

Josh started to protest, but Hickok cut it short.

"You heard me, kid. You reveal the wrong detail, the bosses are going to know they've been bamboozled again. And we could end up feeding those fellas out *there*."

Bill inclined his head toward the vista beyond the open door. In the distance overhead, vultures wheeled like well-oiled mechanisms of death—the frontier's ever-vigilant symbols of a hard fate.

It was a grim view beneath the vultures, too. No homesteads in this Black Hills country, no land under fence. Not even the crude little half-section nester farms Josh had spotted dotting much of the West. Just jaggedly seamed hills covered with dwarf cedars and jackpine, their gullies washed red with eroded soil.

"Does this train go all the way into Deadwood?" Josh asked. When they had laid over at Fort Hammond, in Montana, Bill had pored over the Army's map file of the Black Hills, taking notes.

Bill shook his head. "We'll detrain at Belle Fourche. That's about twenty miles north of Deadwood. We'll follow an old federal freight road. It'll give our horses a chance to stretch out the kinks before we have to board them in a livery again. And us a chance to run our traps."

"Run our traps" was Bill's phrase for gathering information. Josh watched Hickok now thumb his hat back to get a better view of the country hereabouts. The few rough roads they glimpsed were sandy and rocky, with washouts that had to be laboriously detoured.

Erosion dust made the hot air feel gritty and the mouth chalky. Bill tied the neckerchief over his nose and mouth to screen it.

"Bill?"

"Hmm?"

Josh pointed at Hickok's world-renowned, ivory-grip Colt .44 Peacemakers.

"If you can't be Wild Bill in Deadwood, what about them? My grandma could describe those guns."

Bill nodded, crossing to the far corner of the boxcar where they had tossed their saddles and bridles. This half of the car also contained two stalls filled with fresh straw. Bill's strawberry roan and Josh's lineback dun were peacefully enjoying nosebags filled with crushed barley.

Bill untied a buckskin sheath from his pannier. He slid a pump-action shotgun from the sheath. The weapon, manufactured by Spencer Arms Company of Windsor, Connecticut, had a pistol-grip stock of deep-grained walnut.

"I won this little honey a few years back in a poker game up in the Canadian Rockies," Bill explained. "It served me well when I was the star man in Abilene and Hays City. It's my weapon of choice for clearing out choke points."

By "choke points," Josh realized, Bill meant crowd control at close range against saloon ruffians and lynch mobs.

"I'm loading 20-gauge bird shot," Bill added.

"And I've packed the shells with less powder. With bird shot, it's not usually fatal to humans. But I've blinded men with it, and I'll double-dog guarantee you—it's an effective deterrent against bully boys."

And bully boys, Josh knew, were precisely what they were going up against in Deadwood. Pinkerton's information was woefully inadequate to ensure their safety. Nor had Bill told Josh all the details yet. All the reporter knew for sure, right now, was their destination: Harney's Hellhole. The popular name for the most productive gold mine in the Dakotas—and lately, the most ruthless.

"These so-called Regulators," Josh said. "Who do they answer to?"

By long habit, Wild Bill raised a finger to stroke his now missing mustache while he mulled the kid's question. According to Pinkerton, Harney's Hellhole was owned by an international bankers group. It was one of the overseas directors—a Brit—who first contacted Pinkerton about a suspicious rash of "robberies" of gold ore. That same director warned that no one connected with the stateside operation was above suspicion—including the top dogs in management.

"Just who they answer to ain't clear," Bill finally replied. "But sure as Sam Hill, they knew a Pinkerton man when they smelled one, didn't they? Either they're smart as steel traps, or they've got people at the very top. That's what we've got to nose out—just how deep the rot goes and just who we can trust."

By looking hard right out the door, Josh could

barely glimpse the grassy flatland they had crossed to reach this point. Pronghorn antelopes and wild horses moved in herds still visible from the ascending train.

But when he pointed this distant spectacle out to Hickok, Josh noticed something he'd been seeing more frequently of late. Bill looked, all right, turning his gunmetal blue eyes in the direction Josh pointed. However, despite a deep squint, Bill remarked with seeming indifference:

"Can't quite make it out, kid. I must be losing it in the sun."

He's losing it, all right, Josh thought. So far it was only very long distances that gave Bill trouble. But Hickok was starting to lose the one thing he couldn't spare: His hawkeyed vision.

However, Bill derailed Josh's train of thought by suddenly grinning at the reporter.

"What?" Josh demanded defensively.

"Kid, I've let you side me now for over a year. By now I know you've got good leather in you. If not, I'd've sent you home to your Quaker ma by now. But in Deadwood? With that derby hat and square-tipped bow tie, you'll stand out like a rhinestone yo-yo."

"I spoze. Well, should I get duds like yours?"

Bill shook his head. "Nah, just be careful. This time it'll be all right to look like a big-city whippersnapper. Harney's Hellhole is booming right now. Pinkerton says they ain't just desperate for miners and ore freighters—they need clerks that can write and cipher, too. That's where you'll

13

come in. We'll work both sides of the operation, the sweat and the brains."

Josh glanced left out the open door. The front of the train eased into a long S-turn. Josh could see the diamond stack of the locomotive belching black smoke and orange sparks. Streamers of white steam hissed from the escape valves.

"Seems funny," he remarked, "to see silver rails."

This was a steel narrow-gauge railroad, only three feet between rails instead of the usual five. Otherwise a railroad could not have been constructed in this prohibitively expensive terrain. Even now the engineer had to slow way down for a boggy spot that had been reinforced with crushed rock.

"You're going to see plenty of queer sights in the Black Hills," Wild Bill assured him. "This place ain't like nothing else on God's green earth."

Josh could sure believe that. He stared out at the shale-littered slopes of big hills and small mountains. Bright red Indian Paintbrush flowers dotted the lower slopes. They should have seemed like signs of life.

But even those bright daubs of color were all wrong. Josh felt goose bumps forming when he realized why: They looked exactly like blood dotting the landscape.

"This letter is to advise the Indian Bureau," Owen McNulty dictated to his young clerk, "of an extremely dangerous and volatile situation involving

14

the Hunkpapa Sioux at the Copper Mountain Reservation."

"That a *c* or a *k* in Hunkpapa, sir?" the clerk asked.

"A *k*," McNulty replied. He paused in his pacing, listening to the steel nib scratch as Danny Ford, the clerk, caught up. McNulty was in his early fifties, courtly and gaunt. A Methodist preacher who firmly believed red men possessed eternal souls, he had volunteered for the tough job of serving as the Indian agent at Copper Mountain. At times he regretted the idealism that brought him here.

McNulty resumed his pacing. The study was dim save for the circle of light made by Danny's coal-oil lamp. Outside the little clapboard residence, a black-velvet cloak of darkness settled over the *Pahasapa*—the Sioux name for the Black Hills, the sacred center of their universe.

"An alarming number of Indians," McNulty resumed, "are being murdered in cold blood by so-called 'security forces' employed by the mining company in Deadwood. The Sioux have been accused of robbing ore wagons bound for the smelter at Spearfish, South Dakota."

Behind him, Danny's chair made a sudden scraping sound. McNulty, busy composing in his mind, hardly noticed it.

"This accusation against the Sioux," he resumed, "is utterly preposterous. Very few Plains Indians place any value whatsoever on smelted gold, much less raw ore. Even a gold double eagle, to a Sioux, is merely a bauble to sew on one's council shirt."

"Just shows how goddamn hawg-stupid the featherheads are, don't it?"

The sudden, unexpected voice made shock and fear hammer McNulty's temples. He whirled around, then cried out at the horrible scene before him.

"Oh, merciful God! Danny!"

The clerk's steel nib now lay on the puncheon floor in a gathering pool of ink and blood. Danny, a fresh-scrubbed young lad fresh out of high school in Zanesville, Ohio, was slumped dead over his blotter. The bone handle of a knife was centered between his shoulder blades.

"*You!*" McNulty gasped, recognizing the intruder.

"Yeah, it's me, you Indian-loving, God-mongering gal-boy. You had your chance, McNulty. You was warned. You coulda been a rich man just by sticking to your own people. But no, you had to get all sweet on the Noble Red Man, dintcha?"

McNulty backed away, turning pale, as the big intruder stepped closer, wagging a huge Borchardt 44.40 six-shooter equipped with a metal backstrap.

In his shock and confusion, McNulty resorted to officiousness.

"Now see here, Labun. You—you have no authority to enter this house or the reservation. This is all federal property."

"Oh, shucks! There goes *my* spot in heaven, huh?"

"No!" McNulty begged when the man clicked his

hammer back to full cock. It was the loudest, most terrifying sound McNulty had ever heard.

"No?" the intruder repeated, laughing. "I say *yes*, you milk-knee'd Indian lover."

He pulled the trigger. The big pistol exploded with deafening force in the quiet room. McNulty shuddered once as if violently cold. Then his knees came unhinged and he flopped hard onto the floor. His heels scratched the floor for several seconds as his nervous system tried to deny the fact of death.

"*Yes*, you female man," the intruder repeated in a hoarse whisper. "Now that bullet in your belly is federal property too, ain't it?"

Chapter Two

On their first night in South Dakota's Black Hills, Wild Bill and Josh made camp on a bench of grass beside the Belle Fourche River. With trout in every river, walleyes in every reservoir, supper was never a problem in the Dakotas.

Early the next morning, before the August sun began to heat up in earnest, they followed the Old Federal Road south to Deadwood.

"Don't forget we've got summer names," Bill reminded the young reporter when they were only a few miles from town. "I'm Ben Lofley and you're Charlie Mumford. Above all, remember we didn't know each other prior to Deadwood."

Josh nodded, curiously eyeing the hills surrounding them like a pod of whales. Juniper and limber pine covered many of the slopes. This gave them the dark shading, from a distance, that had earned this area its name.

"Where's your pinfire?" Bill asked Josh. Hickok meant the kid's old, but vintage condition, LeFaucheux six-shot pinfire revolver. Bill had given Josh the gun when they first met in Denver. He had also made sure the greenhorn learned how to use it.

"It's in my saddlebag," the kid replied. "I've got an armpit holster. Should I carry it under my shirt?"

Bill shook his head as he skinned back the wrapper of a slim cheroot.

"Leave it where it is," he advised. "Concealed weapons are dicey out West, kid. A man's expected to carry his weapons for the world to see. It's all right for a woman, maybe. But anyhow, a clerk shouldn't carry a gun, open or hidden. They find one on you after you're hired, you'll be up Salt River. Prob'ly kill you for cause on the spot."

This suggestion made Josh's belly stir with apprehension. He let his lineback dun drop back a few more paces, studying the country all around them in pensive silence. Bill covered a sly grin.

Despite their bleak appearance from the railroad train, the Black Hills, Josh soon realized, were abundant with wildlife. Near the numerous streams and ponds he spotted beaver, muskrat, and Great Blue Herons. Golden eagles circled the higher peaks, and mule deer and moose were plentiful in the bottom woods.

Bill held to the point as they ascended a brush-covered bluff. Wind gusts pelted their faces with dust and grit, and both riders pulled up neckerchiefs against it.

Hickok halted at the crest of the bluff and thumbed back his hat for a better view below. Josh hauled up beside him, slacking the reins so his mount could crop grass.

"I dared to dream," Hickok announced with evident sarcasm, "and now it's come true. I'm back in Deadwood."

"Man alive!" Josh's voice was keen with disappointment as he stared at the squalid sight below. "That's *it?*"

Bill snorted. "Longfellow, I've seen some pleasant foothill towns in my time. Deadwood ain't on the list."

Josh stared at rutted, garbage-choked streets and a haphazard collection of hovels and huts. The original mining camp had been established in a saddle between two hills. Now it spilled up the slopes of both hills, spreading like a rash.

"I see there's a few new redbrick buildings since I was here last," Wild Bill remarked. "There's the brick kiln, see it? And that big headframe above it must be Harney's Hellhole."

Even as the two men watched, gunshots and shouting erupted. A mob burst out of a saloon, dragging a struggling man. They tied him behind a horse and whacked it on the butt. The animal bolted, dragging his unfortunate victim along the ground like a loose picket pin.

Josh winced. "He's bouncing over *rocks*, Bill!"

Bill nodded. "Out in Tombstone," he pointed out calmly, "it'd be cactus."

"I wonder what he did?" Josh said.

Bill found this amusing and shook his head. "Kid, you're a caution. He exists, doesn't he? That's a felony in Deadwood."

Josh paled slightly as it finally sank home: In search of an exciting story, he was entering that frontier death trap. A town so risky and dangerous that it humbled even Wild Bill Hickok.

As if reading the kid's thoughts, Bill added: "According to Calamity Jane, I'm going to die down there some day. In the Number 10 Saloon."

"The Number 10?" Josh repeated.

"There's so many saloons in Deadwood," Bill replied, "most with girls in rooms topside, that the owners decided it'd be easier just to number 'em. Daddy Driscoe's Number 10 became the most popular."

Bill pointed to a ramshackle building with water-stained boards.

"That's the feed stable," he told Josh. "You can inquire there about rooms for let. We'll split up now. You ride in from here, I'll circle the bluff and come in from the southeast."

Josh nodded, trying to quell the nervous thudding of his heart. He had faced plenty of trouble at Hickok's side. But now he was riding—alone— into the most dangerous hole in America.

"Since I mentioned the Number 10," Bill added dryly, "let's meet up there later, around nine tonight. At the bar. We'll just be two strangers chewing the fat over a cold beer."

21

"The Number 10?" Josh glanced at his companion. "Tempting fate, are'n'cha?"

Hickok's strong white teeth flashed. "When don't I? You didn't come out here from New York City just to write about a prudent man, now didja?"

Josh grinned back. "Nope," he admitted. "But how did I get in the middle of all the danger?"

"Just lucky, I guess," Bill informed him, kicking his roan into motion.

Cassie Saint John was in a dangerous mood as she reported for work on Monday morning.

Cassie was the wildly popular faro dealer at Deadwood's Number 10 Saloon. The Number 10 had always been fancier and more respectable than the rest of the clapboard-and-canvas watering holes in town. It featured a stair railing of antique brass that wound up toward the rooms of the sporting girls. There were even a few battered billiard tables sporting bullet holes and patched felts.

Cassie sat within a half-circle of clamoring bettors, pretty and proud and demure, while a well-armed case-tender called out each card like a circus barker.

Her foul mood had been triggered by news of the brutal death of her friend Owen McNulty. But as usual, Cassie's outward manner remained calm and benignly indifferent to her seamy surroundings. A thoughtful person, however, might notice that Cassie's little Mona Lisa smile was always restive—as if she were a woman who harbored secret ideas and ambitions.

Just past noon three men, all dressed much better than common miners, entered the Number 10. They took their reserved table at the back of the huge barroom. A Chinese waiter hustled to take their order: three strip steaks, bloody rare, and a pail of cold beer.

Spotting the trio, the bar dog sent a replacement dealer to relieve Cassie. It was tacitly understood that when Deke Stratton, manager of Harney's Hellhole, entered the Number 10, Cassie must be free to join him—if she chose to.

Today she did. All three men stood politely when Cassie approached their table, silk bustle rustling. With Deke were his two most constant companions, Keith Morgan, Mine Captain, and Earl Beckman, chief of company security.

"Cassie," Deke greeted her in his suave Boston baritone. "As usual, you look pretty as four aces."

He drew back a chair for her.

"Always the gentleman, aren't you, Deke?" Cassie murmured as she sat down between Stratton and Beckman.

"Always," Deke assured her with a little ironic smile. "Unless I need to be something else."

Cassie let that comment lie. Deke Stratton was no man's—or woman's—plaything. He had started out in commerce by making a cotton fortune in the rich black soil of east Texas. Stratton quickly learned that money is like manure—it works best when you spread it around. So he went into mining, both investing in and learning the business.

And now look at him. Tailored to the very image of success, with real pearl snaps in his cuffs and a diamond belt buckle worth half the real estate in town. He once told Cassie that if you know how much money you have, you can't be very rich. His singular goal in life was to become so rich that he'd be the most influential private citizen in America.

Cassie, too, burned with ambition. She meant to follow Emerson's advice: "Hitch your wagon to a star." More than once Deke Stratton had parked his boots under her bed.

But right now Cassie ignored her occasional lover. Instead, she turned to Earl Beckman. The former Confederate officer was in his early forties, with a sharp little face like a fox terrier.

"I heard something interesting," Cassie told him, meeting his eyes directly. "A teamster said he saw Merrill Labun heading toward the Copper Mountain Reservation yesterday. Just hours before Owen McNulty and his clerk were murdered."

Beckman blew the head off his beer and took a sip. Then he exchanged brief glances with Stratton and Morgan. Everyone knew that Labun was one of Beckman's favorite dirt-workers.

"Now, now, Miss St. John," Beckman replied in his mellifluous Southern drawl. "You're committing a common fallacy of logic. In Latin it's called *post hoc, ergo prompter hoc*. 'After this, therefore because of this.' There's no proof linking Merrill to the death."

"That's a female for you," Stratton said kindly. "Letting emotions tug them along."

"Sure. It's more likely," chimed in Keith Morgan, a thickset, balding man with a lumpish chin, "that it was redskins that did the dirty deed. Those godless savages probably sacrificed them to their pagan idols."

Cassie glowered at all of them, her pretty face stern with rebuke.

"The Sioux at Copper Mountain admired Owen," she retorted. "And they don't worship idols. They worship the Black Hills—even though they've been stolen from them despite a treaty guarantee."

"The hell's got into you?" Morgan demanded bluntly. "Religion?"

Stratton, however, silenced his subordinate with a glance. Then he looked at Cassie and smiled urbanely. When he spoke, his tone was a thinly disguised warning.

"Friendship is a fine thing, Cassie. I know that you and Owen used to enjoy reading poetry to each other and discussing theater. He was a . . . cultured man."

Morgan started to smirk, but Deke's eyebrows arched and his mouth set itself hard. Morgan coughed to cover his slip.

"Unfortunately," Stratton continued, "South Dakota is no schoolman's Utopia. And Owen could not distinguish between an idealist and a fool. A *fool* may be defined as anyone who lets philosophy hinder profits."

"Meaning what, precisely?" Cassie demanded.

"Well, to give it to you with the bark still on it," Deke clarified, "I mean that Owen was a damn fool."

"So was Don Quixote," Cassie told him evenly. "But I still admire him."

This time when the overseer of Harney's Hellhole spoke, impatience crept into his tone.

"What's done is done. Owen's gone now, and even God can't undo the past. So why keep tilting at windmills, eh?"

Cassie wanted to slap the smooth bastard, but Deke Stratton scared her. She watched him now, gazing around the Number 10 with condescension at all these crude men unfamiliar with opera houses and good grooming.

He seemed to reign over all of them with patrician reserve. And he did own controlling interest in this saloon and several others. But in truth, she knew, Stratton's fatherly mien was deceptive. He could be absolutely ruthless in controlling events for his own benefit.

"I guess you're right, Deke," Cassie relented, prudently giving up for now.

"That's my girl," Stratton assured her. "This world belongs to the living. The dead are just smoke behind us."

Cassie almost choked on his hypocrisy. But fortunately, there was now a diversion unfolding up front. It took Deke's mind off Cassie's dangerously nosy questions.

It all started when the batwings were banged open so hard they almost tore loose from their leather hinges. A stout man wearing greasy teamster's clothing and clumsy hobnail boots stomped in. He clutched the HELP WANTED—ORPHANS PREFERRED sign from the front window.

"My name is Jim Bob Lavoy, and I'm *double* rough!" he roared out. "I triple hog-tie dare *any* of you needle-dicked bug-humpers—'scuze me, ladies—to brace me!"

Everyone, Cassie included, stared in open-mouthed wonder. Despite his greasy, trail-worn appearance, the new arrival wore an immaculate gray John B. Stetson. Nor could Cassie miss the huge Smith & Wesson tied low on his stout thigh.

"You, bar dog!" the man roared out in a voice like gravel scraping. "You lookin' to hire on some help?"

The man behind the bar, Dabney "Dabs" Boudreaux, nodded.

"I could use a nighttime bartender. But this place ain't Fiddler's Green, mister. Can you shoot?"

"Can I shoot? Hell, can the pope pray?"

In an eyeblink the six-shooter filled the stranger's fist. At the first shot, a brass cuspidor on the far side of the barroom leaped into the air.

But that was only the beginning of a remarkable show. In rapid succession he fired his remaining five loads. The cuspidor flew around the periphery of the building, never once touching the floor until all six shots had struck it.

In a civilized city like Denver or St. Louis, such a public display would have landed the marksman in jail. Here in Deadwood, however, it drew an immediate round of applause, cheers, and whistles.

"Hired, by God!" Dabs shouted, and laughter rippled through the saloon.

"Make him wash, though," a miner complained loudly. "He stinks like a dung heap!"

In a heartbeat the new arrival holstered his weapon. With the same movement, he produced a sawed-off pool cue from under his filthy linsey shirt. It *whapped* solidly against the miner's skull, and he toppled like the walls of Jericho.

"You ornery sons of bitches can kill each other for aught I care!" Jim Bob Lavoy called out. "But lay a hand on me, or insult me, and I'll pop you right on the snot locker!"

More laughter and cheers. But now Cassie frowned slightly, noticing something strange about the newcomer. He was stout and strong enough, all right. And obviously he was an ace shooter who could cuss like a trooper.

However, where was his beard—or even the faintest beard shadow? Obviously this "man" hadn't bathed in days, if not weeks—but he had bothered to shave so smoothly? Hardly likely.

Cassie thought again about that remarkable shooting demonstration. That was a trick shooting, not usual survival marksmanship. Suddenly, she had a good idea who this "fellow" was, all right.

But it's none of *my* picnic, she reminded herself. Live and let live, Cassie figured. Her only goal was to enjoy life as much as possible without hurting anyone.

That last thought, however, reminded her of Owen again. Live and let live. . . . Cassie glanced at Deke Stratton. His kind was capable of any abomination for one simple reason: They always hired it out.

As if reading her mind at that very moment, Deke chilled her to her core when he warned her in quiet words: "Don't go tilting at windmills like your hero Don Quixote, Cassie. Around here, that's not just wildly romantic and foolish. It's downright deadly."

Chapter Three

Wild Bill didn't have to worry about drawing attention to himself as he entered Deadwood on horseback. The narrow main street bristled with big, high-wheeled ore wagons pulled by long double teams of mules. These huge conveyance screened a lone rider.

The rammed-dirt sidewalks were crowded with staggering drunks, most of them miners or drifters on the dodge. Vendors hawked everything from matches to Rocky Mountain Oysters—deep-fried bull testicles, a popular and cheap food in mining country.

Bill passed a harness shop, a stage-line office, a myriad of saloons, and an undertaker's parlor—this last quite prominent and prosperous looking. The stench in Deadwood was strong enough to tickle Bill's gag reflex. Chinese workers in floppy blue blouses and long braids hustled to water down the dust choking the streets.

Hickok reined in at the feed stable and turned his roan over to a doltish-looking kid with a big goiter on his neck.

"Curry him good, then grain him," Bill said, flipping the kid a silver dollar. "Don't stall him nights unless the weather's bad. No spurs or whips either. This is a docile animal unless he's mistreated—then he's trained to be a mankiller."

"Yessir, don't you worry none. He'll get treated good here. I like horses a hellva lot better'n I like most folks. No offense meant, sir," he added quickly.

Bill grinned. "None taken, son."

"That there is a fine horse."

Bill nodded, watching him. "What's your name?"

"Lonnie, sir. Lonnie Brubaker."

"No need to call me "sir", Lonnie. I work for my living same as you. The name's Ben. Glad to meetcha."

They shook hands. Wild Bill eyed the young hostler thoughtfully. True, he didn't appear to be the brightest light in town. But Bill's roan was usually a standoffish animal around strangers. Yet, he had instantly taken to the lad and now nuzzled his shoulder. Men good with animals, Bill knew, usually possessed other useful traits, too. And here in Deadwood, Bill needed any help he could get.

Hickok saw Josh's lineback dun in a nearby stall, still feeding. He decided to test this kid.

"I'm looking for a fellow," Bill lied. "Young kid,

little older than you, clean-cut, wears a derby. Seen him? Nuther dollar in it for you."

Bill wanted an element of danger to the question. So he deliberately grabbed his sheathed scattergun as he asked his question. The kid eyed it, swallowing audibly.

"No, sir," he lied right back. And that was exactly the answer Bill wanted to hear. Rather than profit, the kid chose to protect a man from possible wrongdoing. He was a rare thing in this hellhole: decent.

"We'll talk again, Lonnie," Bill promised as he walked off, lugging his gear.

Bill's altered appearance left him feeling somewhat secure from the challenging glares of Deadwood's denizens. Nonetheless, Hickok's first priority was to find a place where he could get off the busy street.

He knew of a big boarding house at the far edge of town, owned by an old trapper's widow named Elsie Nearhood. Hickok stayed there last time he drifted into Deadwood—before he had become a "celebrated frontiersman." And before a grieving father in Texas placed a $10,000 bounty on Bill's life for gunning down his outlaw son.

Wild Bill crossed the street, waiting first to let an ore wagon rattle past, sideboards straining. Above town, on the treeless slopes where men scurried like insects, a huge steam whistle blasted—announcing a shift change at the mine.

Hickok was in luck. Elsie Nearhood was still in business and had one room to let.

"It's itty-bitty," the stout, steel-haired matron

warned him as she led him up a flight of rickety stairs at the rear of the house. "Used to be a servant's quarters. No window, so it gets a mite warm. But I'll knock eight bits a week off your room and board, Benjamin."

The room Elsie showed him was hardly more than a cubbyhole. A pedestal washstand with a metal pitcher and bowl, a crude bed of leather webbing, and one ladderback chair comprised the furnishings. Several nails in one wall took the place of a closet.

"Looks fine," Bill said stoically, paying her for two weeks in advance.

"No women up here," Elsie added when the money was already in her pocket.

Bill grinned. "Where would I put 'em in this packing crate?"

Elsie was talkative and prone to gossip. Bill needed to get a sense for the way the townies felt about Harney's Hellhole and the men who ran it. Back downstairs in her parlor, as Elsie wrote out Bill's receipt, he remarked casually:

"I'm planning on applying at the mine for work. Think they're hiring?"

"Oh, you'll get on," she assured him. "If you're that crazy to want to. That old hellhole kills men about as quick as the big nabobs can hire them. Matter-of-fact, that's why I've got a room empty."

"Mining ain't for nervous nellies, Mrs. Nearhood. It's dangerous work."

"Mmm. Especially around here."

"How so?" Bill asked, keeping his voice only casually curious.

Elsie sniffed. "Well now, Benjamin Lofley, I'm not one of these ingrates who mean-mouth the company while growing fat off it. Harney's Hell-hole has made Deadwood a boomtown for everybody. My lands, even the Chinee and the Mexer can afford fripperies these days. Still . . ."

Elsie glanced around the parlor as she handed him his receipt. Though they were alone, she lowered her voice.

"Still . . . there's some as think they're gods. Gods made of gold. And now that nice Owen McNulty's been murdered. Oh yes, mining is dangerous work. And so is defying those who run the mines."

Elsie hushed herself up, realizing she was being indiscreet. But Hickok felt a little jolt of shock move through him when she pronounced the name of McNulty. Murdered! The Indian agent's name had been on the very short list of local contacts Pinkerton said Bill could trust.

Just then Hickok realized Elsie was scrutinizing his face, her blunt features squinched in concentration.

"You sure do look familiar," she mused.

Only now did Wild Bill spot it, tacked onto the faded, rose-pattern wallpaper behind Elsie: his own mustachioed face and gunmetal blue eyes, staring off the cover of *Harper's Weekly*.

Elsie caught him staring at it.

"That's Wild Bill Hickok," she informed him proudly. "He stayed here once, back in the sixties after the war. We all called him J. B. then."

"Do tell? Hickok, huh? You know, I hear he's

quite the fashion dandy." Bill said this to empha-
size his own drab, workaday appearance.

"Dandy? Huh! Why, he was downright wom-
anish about his appearance," Elsie insisted. "And
perfumed? My hand to God, the man smelled like
a French you-know-what."

Bill barely stopped himself from frowning. He
did tend to favor some fine colognes. "That bad,
huh?"

"Ben, he *smelled* like a woman. And from behind, he looked like a woman. All them blond
curls, lordy! Made me wonder if maybe Mrs.
Hickok had wanted a daughter 'stead of a son.
Maybe raised him up to be a gal-boy?"

The heat of indignation came into Bill's face.
Steady, hoss, he warned himself.

"Now Elsie, he must be all man and then some,"
Wild Bill argued, forcing the defensiveness from
his tone. "I mean, I hear he's always with a beautiful woman."

"Why sure, that's how he gets his perfumes," Elsie pointed out. "I have my doubts about him, famous or no. A man should *look* like a man."

Why, you old bat, Bill thought. But Hickok decided not to push his luck with any more questions. He quickly stowed his gear in his tiny room,
cleaned up a little, then searched out a café and
enjoyed a steak dinner with all the trimmings.

But as he lingered over berry pie and coffee, Elsie Nearhood's words echoed in memory: *There's
some as think they're gods. Gods made of gold.*

*   *   *

35

Toward the middle of the afternoon, Bill inquired where to find the mine's hiring office. Even with his sheathed scattergun in one hand, Bill felt naked without his sidearms. He followed a well-worn path toward a tar-paper shack. The single word JOBS had been whitewashed over the door.

The noise grew louder as he ascended. Steam pumps steadily clanked and hissed, keeping down the water level in the underground stopes where the miners labored.

The days of easy panning and hydraulic mining were gone. All color now was deep down in the bedrock. Here and there Bill saw shaft-houses rising up from the ground like big outhouses. These contained the skips that took men down into the stopes.

Bill watched a group of miners pile onto one of the skips. All of them had unnaturally pale skin and wore clothing streaked red with clay and pigments. Their helmets had fat candles mounted in front.

A bell clanged, the hoist man hit a lever, and steam escaped in an airy sigh. The huge hoist wheel turned and down they all went, as if swallowed by the bowels of the earth.

"Form a straight line, you flea-bitten shitheels!" a man's voice brayed out nearby. "If you're drunk, get the hell outta here! No cripples and no men over forty-five! You must also pass a lifting test to check for hernias."

Outside the hiring office, Bill saw a big, barrel-chested man with a star pinned to his rawhide vest. He was built like a granite block. Part of the company's private security force. Bill eyed the blacksnake whip he carried coiled in his left hand. A Borchardt 44.40 with a metal backstrap bulged from his hand-tooled holster.

"I said a *line*, not a goddamn cluster!" he roared out. "You're a mob! You want a job here, you best learn to take orders."

Bill took his place in line. It moved along fairly briskly. Every two minutes or so another man emerged from the shack. Most of them, Bill noticed, clutched a new hiring contract. Again he recalled Elsie's words: *That old hellhole kills men about as quick as the big nabobs can hire them.*

Bill glanced at the bully boy with the badge. It's not just the mine that's killing them, he speculated.

Unfortunately, the thug looked right at Bill before he could avert his eyes. The big man charged Bill's position.

"You sweet on me, mister?" the man demanded. "Hey? Are you?"

"No, sir," Bill snapped back.

His "sir" seemed to mollify the bully somewhat. Or so he pretended, thought Bill.

"Then don't be staring," he said in a quieter voice. "And when you step inside, you leave that smoke pole by the door."

"Yessir," Bill responded with military precision.

The bully boy took in his relatively clean grooming and noticed there was no liquor smell on this applicant's breath.

"Mind your pints and quarts around here," the man confided in an almost friendly tone, "and you'll move up fast. You look like a man with some mettle in him."

The security man moved off, while Bill inched up steadily closer to the door. The afternoon waned and the shadows began to lengthen. From where he stood he could see how the surrounding slopes were chockablock with more tar-papered shacks—provided by the company for the married miners.

Finally it was Bill's turn to step inside. He grounded his weapon, then took up a respectful parade rest position in front of a crude deal desk.

A skinny man, with impatient eyes and a cigarette dangling from his lips, sat behind the desk. A powder keg served as his chair. Not only was there an American flag in a standard behind him, but another on a little pin in his lapel. The bully boy outside wore one too. Patriotism, Bill reminded himself—the last refuge of a scoundrel.

The hiring officer gave Bill a quick once-over.

"Ever worked in a gold mine before?" he demanded.

"Yessir. Up on the Comstock."

Bill meant the Comstock Lode, a rich deposit of silver and gold ore discovered near Virginia City, Nevada, by Henry T. P. Comstock. Bill did indeed work there for a year, but as a guard for the ore trains.

"What job?" the hiring boss demanded.

Bill almost grinned at the irony. In fact it was the security forces that Bill hoped to infiltrate. But he dare not request such an assignment—not with three other Pinkertons known to have done the same.

So Bill lied through his teeth.

"I started out as a toss man on the slusher line, sir. Worked my way up to crew chief in seven months."

This news seemed to chase the impatience from the other man's eyes. The slusher line was an important part of any mining operation. High-grade ore formed veins in rocks, veins that could be detected by a trained eye. A "toss man" had the tough and dangerous job of riding along on the huge slusher buckets, the receptacles that held the waste materials mucked out from the stopes below. He had to quickly sort through the material and toss out any valuable ore before it was dumped into a waste pit. The job was important and paid more than most mining jobs.

The hiring boss sized up Bill again.

"You ain't a 'specially big man, Ben. It's usually big fellas on the slusher line. Let me see you lift that."

He pointed toward a good-sized boulder that rested to the left of his desk. Men were required to lift it as proof they did not have debilitating hernias—a serious problem on the frontier.

Bill squatted and lifted it with evident ease.

The boss's strong stern face cracked into a smile. "Hell, you're strong as horseradish, fellow! Say you know the business, hanh?"

In truth, Wild Bill Hickok would rather face great danger than hard physical labor. He had never actually worked in a mine.

But he paid close attention, and he had learned plenty of key terms like "angle of repose" and "ore gradients." Hickok was a quick study with other details, too. Now he was able to talk about stopes and drifts and tipples, pumps and ores and underground surveying, with the appearance of some knowledge.

As a result he was hired on as a crew chief, his salary $2.75 per day instead of the usual $2.00 for common labor.

"The job pays in Eastern money," the mining official explained. He meant paper banknotes instead of gold or silver coins. "Any problem with that?"

Bill shrugged. "No, sir. Some don't trust paper, but I figure it all spends the same."

"You got a healthy attitude, Ben," the other man praised, chuckling. "Most of them whine like women."

Since he had to start work at sunup tomorrow, Bill knew he'd better make sure to meet up with Josh later tonight at the Number 10. He needed to find out if the kid got hired and where he was staying.

"Merrill?" the hiring boss shouted while Bill was signing his contract.

The big security man with the whip poked his head inside. "Yeah?"

"Merrill, this is Ben Lofley. He's going to be taking over the slusher crew, starting tomorrow. Ben, meet Merrill Labun. He's next in line after our security chief, Earl Beckman. You'll meet Mr. Beckman and the rest of the mine officers in good time."

Bill and Labun exchanged nods.

"A man who keeps himself squared away," the hiring boss added, "can find himself eventually rolling in it. This mine has almost surpassed the Homestead Mine in overall production. In fact we'd hold the record if not for the ore we've had robbed, which doesn't count in production figures."

At this last remark, Labun glanced out the door. Bill could have sworn the man started to smile. Hickok's eyes fell to the fancy metal backstrap on Labun's .44. That was a special issue gun for Cavalry NCO's.

"But I should also warn you, Ben," the hiring boss said, "that Merrill and his boys run a tight ship around here."

Labun met Bill's eyes again and nodded. "That's right. Good workers got nothing to fear. But any nail that sticks up *will* get hammered down hard."

Chapter Four

Bill returned to his shoebox-size room, dropped the bar across the door, and slept the sleep of the just for the next few hours. He woke up too late for the evening meal provided by Elsie. So he decided to wait and grab something at the Number 10 when he met Josh.

Except for the saloons, most Western towns folded up at sunset. But the booming mine employed night crews to load ore wagons. Even at 9 P.M. Bill was forced to dodge wagon traffic when he crossed the street. Golden light spilled out from the crowded Number 10, along with a jumbled racket of shouts, laughter, curses, and a tinkle of player-piano notes.

Hickok settled the floppy-brimmed plainsman's hat lower on his head, casting much of his smooth-shaven face in shadow. He couldn't help a queasy churning of his stomach as he approached the batwings of the Number 10.

Foolish superstition or not, the prophecy of his own death made Bill look at the place differently. And right now he was virtually defenseless—he had left even his scattergun in his room.

However, before he even went inside, Bill spotted Josh in the street outside the saloon. He milled among a growing throng of men and boys gathering around a huge conveyance drawn by a pair of mules. The team was festooned with garlands of papier-mâché flowers.

The vehicle was completely enclosed like a paddy wagon. Light from the Number 10 splashed on its gaudily painted sideboards: SEE THE MIRAKULUSS ROLLING ROCK!!!

"*Step* right up close, gentlemen, that's the ticket!" barked a hatchet-faced man wearing a straw boater. He stood on the rig's board seat. "Friends, for a mere five cents you can view the very stone that covered our Lord's tomb! On loan to me by special arrangement with Saint Peter's Basilica in Rome, Italy."

Bill sniggered, immediately recognizing the same grifter he had once seen working a scam in Sioux City. Only, that time, the con man was selling numbered chunks of wood "from the very cross on which the Lord was crucified."

"That's it, chappies, and don't be afrighted when you see how it *glows in the dark*. It is merely radiating the spirit of the Nazarene himself! Just one-twentieth of a dollar, gentlemen, to witness a bona fide, by-God miracle!"

Shaking his head, Wild Bill watched Josh pay his nickel and file into the wagon. And that kid bragged about going to high school!

Hickok slapped the batwings and entered the Number 10. The place was so busy that three bartenders were kept hopping behind the long, S-shaped counter.

Keeping his eyes slanted toward the floor, yet carefully studying the interior, Hickok began nudging his way toward an open spot at the bar. Already he had spotted big Merrill Labun, matching shots of whiskey with another man at a table along a side wall.

Bill ordered a shot of Old Taylor bourbon, a schooner of beer to chase it, and some boiled eggs to quell the hunger gnawing at his belly. He was peeling the second egg when Josh, pretending to ignore him, pushed into the spot beside Bill. Like Bill, he lifted one foot onto the brass floor rail that ran the length of the bar.

Hickok spoke low without turning his head. "Get your nickel's worth outside, chawbacon?"

"Ahhh." Josh's tone was embarrassed. "I knew it was all a hoodwink. But how does he make that stone glow in the dark? It really did. I saw it."

"I've seen this scam before. The stone's coated with dust from a spot near Taos in the New Mexico Territory," Bill replied. "Indians call the spot Burning Sands. Nobody knows why, but this dust gives off a green glow in the dark. Some think it's a new ore we don't know about yet."

Bill slid a cheroot from his shirt pocket, still ig-

44

noring the kid. "How'd you make out today? Get a job?"

"Man alive, did I ever. You were right, Bill. Clerks are scarce out here. When I told them I can translate French and German, they hired me at twice a common miner's wage. The mine is an international concern, and they need a foreign correspondence clerk. That's me."

Twice the common wage, Bill thought with a sting of envy. That meant Josh was getting four dollars a day! A buck and a quarter more than he himself was getting as a crew chief.

"Get a room?" Bill asked.

"They told me not to stay in town. I guess clerks get roughed up a lot. The clerical staff are provided a clean bed in a worker's dormitory the company runs. I can come and go as I please during off hours. I work the same hours as the miners, sunup to sunset five days a week with two thirty-minute meal breaks. Half a day on Saturday, Sundays off."

While Josh spoke, Bill had idly been watching a big knot of bettors crowd the faro table. Now, as the knot momentarily parted, he realized what the big attraction was: the beautiful blonde with the huge, sea-green eyes who was dealing.

Now *she's* right out of the top drawer, Hickok told himself, suddenly alerting to a quality female like a hound on point.

"I been asking some questions without being too obvious," Josh said. He spoke with his glass held to hide his lips and looked straight ahead into the back-bar mirror. "Deke Stratton is lots more than just a mine operator. He owns controlling interest in almost every business in Deadwood. He also controls the townsite charter."

"Yeah, I figured that out already. That's why the mine's private police force also serves as the only legal authority in town. I noticed when I rode in: No sheriff's office or jailhouse or courthouse."

Josh nodded.

"You know what Stratton looks like?" Bill asked.

"I met him briefly when they were showing me the front offices. Seemed friendly enough. He's got real facility with a cliché. He could get on in politics. He's here tonight, by the way."

"*Don't* point, you soft brain," Hickok snapped. "And don't turn around. Use the mirror."

"Oops, sorry. He's the tall, well-dressed one among the three at the table in the back," Josh explained. "Earlier, the faro dealer joined them for a drink. Stratton's pretty free about touching her."

"Interesting," Bill muttered. "But not surprising."

He studied all three men. They were somewhat distorted in the smoke-filmed, warped mirror.

"Who're the other two?" Bill asked.

"The bald fellow with the lumpy chin is Keith Morgan, the Mine Captain. He's also an expert in demolitions. One of the accounting clerks told me he was a famous sapper with Robert E. Lee's Army of Northern Virginia. He—"

Bill suddenly swore, interrupting Josh. "Morgan, you say? Well, cuss my coup, kid! You must mean the Reb devil we called 'Boomer' Morgan. We named him that 'cause his explosions were always big and loud. Christ, he once tunneled up under an infantry company and blew away two hundred men in their sleep."

"No kidding? Well, judging from his manner today, Morgan is a pig," Josh reported bluntly. "But the other fellow, Earl Beckman, wasn't a bad sort. He's the Security Chief. When he found out I read French, he started discussing—quite intelligently—the novels of Balzac."

Bill snorted beer foam out his nose. "Balzac, my sweet aunt! Listen, I've met rapists who can quote Shakespeare, kid. Don't confuse learning with decency. If Beckman is the security chief at Harney's Hellhole, I'll guarantee you his hands are bloody."

"Yeah," Josh conceded. "Speaking of bloody . . . have you heard that the Indian agent was murdered? Owen McNulty?"

Bill nodded. "Whether they want to or not, looks like the local Sioux figure into the mix, too. We'll have to talk to them as soon as we can."

For a moment, something about the stout bartender at the far end of the counter caught Bill's notice. That gray Stetson, it seemed familiar somehow. . . .

A little prickle of alarm tickled his scalp. That gray Stetson . . . but before Bill could solidify the thought, the stunning faro dealer again caught his attention.

In the mirror, he watched her remove a cigarette from a slim gold case. She pulled it through a hole drilled into a gold coin, packing the tobacco before she inserted the cigarette into an ivory holder.

47

That's no soiled dove who makes trips upstairs, Bill realized. There were really only two social classes in the frontier West: the Quality and the Equality. She was definitely Quality.

For a moment Bill felt her glance touch him and move away. It would have lingered, he reminded himself, if she knew who he really was. He was no longer the center of attention, just another common roustabout with his pants worn to a shine. Now that he couldn't count on it, Bill sorely missed his fame.

"Listen, Joshua," Bill said, still watching the faro dealer in the mirror, "I want you to be good to that simpleton-looking kid at the livery. Lonnie Brubaker."

"Why?"

"I want him on our side. He's in a good position to notice a lot. And he's not likely to be seen as a threat by anybody. We might have to communicate through him if things heat up."

But in fact, Bill realized, things were heating up right now. Merrill Labun, with his drunken friend in tow, was headed toward Hickok's spot at the bar. Bill recalled Labun's odd behavior earlier, at the hiring office, when he had abruptly changed his bullying manner to one of gruff friendliness. The thug was up to something.

"Stand by," he warned Josh. "And remember we're not together. If all hell breaks loose, *don't* back me."

"Howdy, Ben," Merrill Labun greeted Bill, giving him a hearty whack on the back. "Ben, meet one of our security men, Danny Stone. Danny, this

48

is Ben Lofton, our new slusher line crew chief."

"It's Lofley, Mr. Labun," Bill corrected him politely, sensing that Labun's "mistake" was fully intended. "Not Lofton."

"Sure, sure. Sorry, bud. Ben here is real polite and squared away, Danny. Called me 'sir.'"

"Do tell? Now where I come from, politeness is all right for women and weak men."

Stone, too, was a big man, thick in the shoulders and chest. He gave the smaller, more slightly built Hickok a sneering once-over.

"Maybe he was a soldier boy?" Stone suggested. "See how he's got—whatchacallit?—military bearing? Did you go for a soldier, Lofton?"

"Lofley," Bill repeated quietly. He finished his beer and set the heavy schooner down. But Hickok kept his fingers wrapped around the thick handle. "Yes, I served."

"You fight in the war?" Stone demanded.

"Which one, friend? I believe there's been several."

"Which one?" Stone snarled. "Ain't *he* the big war chief! I'm talking about *the* war, you damned blockhead! The one to whip the Yankees."

This last comment came out loud and belligerent. The men nearby turned to watch and listen. Many had instantly taken the quiet stranger's side—Stone was too far north to openly brag about whipping Yankees.

"I fought in that one," Bill confirmed. "But I was on the side that dictated your surrender."

Hickok chose that goading answer carefully, realizing this highly public moment was a crucial test of his authority. An authority he must establish quickly if he meant to infiltrate the illegal operation at its core. Even without his famous .44s, *this* was the crucial moment to follow his credo: *Shoot first, ask questions later.*

"Oh, you did, huh?" Stone's breath reeked of rotgut whiskey as he pushed up against Hickok. "You know what that makes you, blue belly? A goddamn stinking—*uuh!*"

Bill put all of his considerable upper-body strength into a swing with the schooner. It struck with a sickening thud, smashing across the bridge of Stone's nose. He loosed a bray of pain, and Bill watched his eyes lose their focus.

A heartbeat later, Stone was an unconscious, bleeding heap on the floor.

The entire saloon seemed to hold its collective breath, waiting to see what Labun would do. After all, the quiet stranger in the floppy black hat had just coldcocked a security man—the same as assaulting a law officer, in these parts.

For a long moment Labun just stood there, fingering the heavy brass studs on his belt. Then he grinned at Bill.

"Hell, Danny gets a little rowdy when he's had a skinful. He's a former miner himself. They're a scrappy bunch. But he won't hold a grudge when he sobers up, Ben."

The tension had built up inside Bill like a coiled spring. Now he released it in a long sigh. He shrugged.

"Scratch a miner and you'll find a brawler," he said quietly. "No harm done."

"You're a good man, Ben," Labun said, thumping him again. "See you tomorrow at work."

Labun recruited a few helpers and hauled his still-dazed comrade from the saloon. Fights were as common as cockroaches in Deadwood, and almost immediately this brief encounter was forgotten. But Hickok felt the faro dealer's seawater eyes linger on him this time, as if taking his measure.

"Good work, Bill," Josh praised him in low tones. "Looks like you've made a good impression on the very people we need to fool most."

"You start thinking that way," Wild Bill warned the youth, "and we'll both end up wearing those suits with no back in them."

"But you just saw—"

"Stick your 'buts' back in your pocket," Bill cut him off. "I think I convinced the hiring boss today, sure. But the security crew must be on guard for more infiltrators. Merrill got a little too friendly all of a sudden. He might be setting me up, testing me."

Bill decided it was time to turn in. Sunup would come around damn quick, and he had some hard labor ahead of him. Labor he was not conditioned for.

As he turned to leave, however, Wild Bill again noticed that stout bartender in the gray Stetson. And this time, the bartender was studying him right back.

By Godfrey, Calamity Jane told herself, that *is* Wild Bill, sure as cats fighting.

"Hey, Jim Bob!" demanded a miner in red-stained work clothes. "You work here or just visiting? I ordered a goddamn beer!"

"Order it in hell, you loudmouthed peckerwood," Jane shot back, sliding a beer toward him along the counter.

"Tell me something," the miner added when he was safely out of range—a sawed-off pool cue dangled by a thong from one of the bartender's wrists. "Did a plow do that to your face, or was you just borned ugly?"

"Your scrotum will make my next ammo pouch," Jane promised in her rusty voice. The miner wisely faded into the crowd.

Calamity Jane watched, her heart sitting out a few beats, as the love of her life made his way out the door.

Yes, it *had* to be Wild Bill! There was Joshua Robinson trailing out, too—that cute little newspaper fellow who tailed Bill like a shadow. Clearly Hickok was in Deadwood under a summer name, and Jane knew why.

Indeed, that's why she was here right now, her hair shorn off to pass for a man. Lately, every newspaper in the country was covering news out of the Black Hills Badlands. Why? A hunch had told her Wild Bill Hickok would be dusting his hocks in this direction. And that hunch panned gold.

"I said *whiskey!*" snarled a voice in Jane's ear. "You deaf or what?"

An angry, beefy-faced crew foreman glowered at her.

"*Here's* your goldang whiskey, liver lips," Jane replied, smashing a half-filled bottle of Old Crow over his head. Two Chinese employees promptly hustled over to drag the unconscious man outside.

Of all the dangerous watering holes on the vast frontier, thought Jane, this was the one she dreaded most. For Bill's sake, not her own. That ancient palmist down in Old El Paso was the best in Mexico. And she had assured Jane, even swearing it on the Holy Bible, that Wild Bill Hickok would be killed at the Number 10 saloon in Deadwood. An astrological doctor in Amarillo confirmed that prediction.

When would the black deed happen? That question Jane could not answer. And perhaps—especially if the Creator's hand was in it—she couldn't do one thing to prevent it. But J. B. Hickok, in Jane's lovestruck opinion, was one of the only true men in America. And those gun-barrel blue, direct-as-searchlight eyes of his . . . why, Jane felt loin warmth just *thinking* about that purty critter.

"A sarsaparilla for Cassie, Jim Bob," called out the case-tender from the faro table.

Jane scowled as she pulled a bottle from a hogshead of ice behind her. She poured the soda pop into a tall glass for the pretty faro dealer. Jane had noticed the attractive blonde eyeballing Bill after he dropped that big security man in his tracks. Even shorn of his good looks, that man attracted comely gals like iron filings to a magnet.

But never mind her jealousy. Jane was here in Deadwood to watch over Wild Bill. Hickok might die anytime now—but God better save a place in hell, Jane vowed, for any son of a bitch who harmed her Billy.

Chapter Five

A man's voice, deep and wildly off-key, sang loud
enough to send his words echoing through the
hills and low mountains:

And the moonbeams lit
On the tipple of her nit. . . .

It was just past forenoon. Already the August
day was hot and windless. The terrain hereabouts
was mostly scrub cottonwood and dwarf cedars.
The hillsides were dotted with wilted bluebonnets
and daisies dying in the heat.

"Aww, hell. Just one more nip to wash my
teeth," Butch Winkler told his favorite mule.

Butch, a big and affable teamster wearing buckskin clothing, used his few remaining teeth to pull
the cork from a bottle of 40-rod. He was heading
toward the big ore smelter at Spearfish, northeast
of Deadwood. Harney's Hellhole, like most of the

55

new underground mines, was not equipped for the complex mercury-separation process required to remove gold from rocks.

While the miles dragged slowly by, Butch accompanied himself on a banjo. Now and then he scanned the bleak countryside, on the watch for trouble. He couldn't understand why so many ore wagons had been attacked and stolen lately—especially, so the rumors went, by Sioux Indians.

Gold ore was virtually worthless even to white thieves much less red ones. Only big corporations could afford to pay the huge fees for smelting and mercury separation. Another thing Butch couldn't puzzle out: With so many wagons heisted lately, why wasn't the company sending armed guards to side the wagons? Hell, you'd almost think they *wanted* to get robbed.

"I'm just a stupid mule whacker," Butch told the beast he was riding. "The hell do *I* know? The rich man says 'hawk,' and I spit—which I could . . ."

Fwip!

The arrow that suddenly punched into the left side of Butch's neck pushed a streaming arc of blood and tissue out the right side. The big man swayed, choking on his own blood. A few moments after he was struck, he slid heavily to the ground. Butch's unfired Spencer carbine was still slung over his right shoulder.

"Good eye," Danny Stone praised when the arrow shot by Merrill Labun skewered its target. "You're gettin' to be a reg'lar red warrior, boss."

Labun grinned as he hung the osage wood bow

back on his saddle horn. He had made sure to use an arrow fletched with black crow feathers. Most Sioux Indians used white feathers except those nearby at Copper Mountain. They had adopted black feathers from their Cheyenne cousins, who were now completely driven from this area.

"C'mon," Labun said, kicking his horse forward down the slope. "Let's get this wagon headed toward Devil's Tower before somebody comes along."

A third man accompanied them as they rode down to the trail. He was dressed like a typical teamster in buckskin shirt and trousers with a floppy-brim hat.

"Now remember, Steve," Labun told the new driver. "Anybody asks, you're under contract to the Liberty Mining Company. This ore did *not* come from Harney's Hellhole. It's from the Phelps-Landau Mine near Rapid City."

By now the trio had reached the trail below. They dismounted, hobbled their horses, then set to work.

Butch Winkler's body was unceremoniously dumped beside the trail. The task of taking the scalp fell to Stone. He made the outline cut with his skinning knife. Then he placed one knee on the corpse's neck and gave a sharp tug to the scalp. It came off with a ripping sound like bubbles popping.

"Damn," Steve said, averting his eyes. "That's disgusting."

Merrill, meantime, took the sheaf of load papers from the dead man's legging sash. These included the scale weight of the wagon as well as both the origin and destination of the load.

Labun removed a phosphor from his pocket and scratched it to life with his thumbnail. He burned the original load papers, then handed Steve a new counterfeit set.

"You're sure you know the trail to the smelter at Devil's Tower?" Labun asked the driver. This was Steve's first ore-wagon heist.

Steve nodded. "I just follow the old Sundance Road, then take the cutoff at Bear Lodge Mountain."

" 'At's it. The Phelps-Landau Mine has all but played out," Labun explained. "And most people know that at the Spearfish smelter. But we've got men in key jobs at Devil's Tower. No questions will be asked."

Devil's Tower was located in Wyoming's northeast corner. A massive cluster of rock columns rising about 1,300 feet into the air. Located at the border where the mining country ended and the Thunder Basin Grassland began, it was an ideal location for a smelter.

"What I can't figure," Danny Stone chimed in, "is why more people aren't asking *why* Indians would steal gold ore? I mean, don't nobody wonder what primitive, gut-eating savages even do with it?"

Danny's voice was affected by the tape across his broken nose, the legacy of his encounter last night with Ben Lofley, the new guy.

Labun snorted. "Christ, you sound just like Earl. He's so worried about that he wants us to start faking Indian raids. Yipping, wearing feathers, the whole shebang. I say who *cares* how it looks to some?"

Labun pointed to the last ashes of the papers he had just burned; they scattered in a puff of wind.

"The Army was practically demobilized after the war," Labun reminded his toady. "Hell, there's only 1,500 soldiers to cover the entire frontier. And there's only one U.S. marshal in this area. He don't matter on account he's on Deke's payroll. Truth to tell, ain't nobody who much cares what goes on in this God-forgotten territory."

"Nobody except whoever's paying Allan Pinkerton," Danny reminded him.

"True, but I'd wager they've given that up. So does Earl. Hell, we've put the quietus on three of Pinkerton's men."

"I still think this Ben Lofley bears watching," Danny insisted.

"Sure you do—he busted your snot locker for you. But don't sweat, old son, I am watching him."

By now Steve had transferred his personal gear to the ore wagon and mounted the lead mule. He lashed the teams into motion with a light sisal whip.

"Remember," Labun called out to him. "The gold is to be credited to the Liberty Mining Company."

"Keep an eye out for wild Indians," Danny added, and all three men laughed.

At 11 A.M. a steam whistle announced the day's first half-hour break. Hickok, who had been busting his hump nonstop for five hours, simply collapsed on the ground outside the headframe of the mine. He was too damned tired to bother eating the roast-beef sandwich and fruit that Elsie packed for all her lodgers working at the mine.

Although he was a crew chief, Bill was required to work just like the other two dozen men on the slusher line. And mining work, he quickly realized, required the endurance of a doorknob.

"Tuckered out, boss?" called out a friendly Welshman everybody called Taffy.

"Worn down to the hubs," Bill conceded. "Gonna take me awhile to get the right muscles broke in again."

"So why in Sam Hill are *you* crew chief, Lofley?" demanded a burly man with forearms like bowling pins. "I been tossin' ore for a year now."

The speaker was Brennan O'Riley, a surly Irishman who had taken an instant dislike to his new boss. Bill watched him devour a huge doughnut in one bite.

"Damned if I know," Bill replied, massaging his sore arms. "I just asked for a job."

"Tain't fair," O'Riley insisted. "It's like stealing money from a man's pocket."

Bill was too damned tired for a confrontation. He glanced around at the slusher crew as they lay sprawled on the grassless slope. Most of them wore Levi Strauss's blue jeans with the new copper-riveted pockets that made them ideal for hard work like mining.

Many of these miners had been saddle tramps previously and would be again if they survived

Harney's Hellhole. Others were veterans of the great war. They found this back-breaking labor a good antidote to their nightmare memories.

"Over yonder comes the big bosses," Taffy remarked. Bill looked where Taffy pointed—Deke Stratton and Earl Beckman were crossing from the main office toward the mine area.

But Hickok had to squint hard to recognize them at this distance. And squinting, he told himself, was something he'd done plenty lately. No man welcomed the failing of his eyes—but Hickok knew that, for a gunman, it was a death sentence.

"That goldang Stratton already owns most of Deadwood," another miner remarked. "Now I hear he's even opened up a law office in Rapid City so he can profit off the divorce trade."

Bill laughed although it was no joke. The "divorce trade" had become the only other real industry in mining country. Western states were unburdened by the strict morality back east in the Land of Steady Habits. They were actually courting the out-of-state divorce trade, even running big ads in Eastern newspapers. Utah and the Dakotas, especially, had gained celebrity as divorce mills.

"What I hear he's 'getting into,'" O'Riley tossed in, "is Cassie Saint John."

His bawdy remark triggered laughter on the slope. Meantime, Stratton and Beckman were drawing closer. Stratton was hatless and wore a vermilion ranch suit. Beckman wore a felt campaign hat and neat starched khakis, his badge glinting in the sun.

Again the steam whistle blasted, announcing the end of the morning break. The slusher line— a thick steel cable with big metal muck buckets hanging at fifteen-foot intervals—shimmied and groaned as it started up again.

"Time to hit it, boys," Wild Bill called out. His muscles screamed in protest when he stood up.

The men all lined up at the "jump station," a spot just outside the mine entrance. Each man hopped into a muck bucket as it eased slowly out of the mine. Each worker had about three minutes to sort through the waste material, tossing any valuable ore out. Then he had to leap out only seconds before the buckets swung out over a vast waste pit. A fixed grapple caught a hook on each bucket and opened it to dump the contents.

"O'Riley!" Bill snapped out. "*Every* man to the jump station."

Brennan O'Riley had just begun a huge hunk of blackberry cobbler when the whistle sounded. Now he lingered on the slope to finish it.

O'Riley deliberately ignored his new crew chief, smacking his lips and licking his fingers.

"O'Riley!" Bill shouted a second time. "You bolted to that spot? Get to work!"

"Blow it out your bunghole," the big man snarled, though he did finally rise and amble up to the jump station.

Bill caught the edge of a bucket, swung in, and began sorting through the muck. By now Deke Stratton and Earl Beckman had paused to watch the slusher-line crew in action.

Hickok had noticed, all morning long, that

O'Riley was a lazy worker—the real reason why he had never made crew chief. He tended to toss out too many worthless rocks, which meant he was also leaving good ore to waste. O'Riley also liked to leap out of the bucket early so he didn't have so far to walk back.

So far, though, Bill had said nothing. But now, with Stratton and Beckman on hand, was a good time to act.

"O'Riley," he said next time the two men were waiting for a bucket, "I want you to toss out gold, not rocks. And don't leave the bucket until it reaches the pit."

"I don't give a big one *what* you want, Lofley," O'Riley growled. "You damned Johnny-come-lately pipsqueak."

O'Riley folded his brawny arms over his chest, staring belligerently at his boss. Hickok could feel Stratton's eyes on him, gauging how he handled this.

"You're docked one day's pay," Bill announced. "You keep on malingering, I'm firing you."

Rage smoldered in O'Riley's eyes. "Fire a cat's tail, you skinny piece of crap."

"That's it," Bill told him. He pointed at the office with his thumb. "You're canned, mister. Go draw your pay and then clear off the property."

"Suits me fine. But first me and you are going to waltz, boss man."

O'Riley lunged at the smaller man, sending a looping blow toward his jaw. That blow would have knocked Bill out cold if he had not easily sidestepped it.

Hickok was a shooter, not a brawler. He could not afford to trade blows with a man-mountain like Brennan O'Riley. So instead the lithe and agile Hickok counted on fancy footwork and a series of fast, well-aimed blows.

Once, twice, again, yet again Hickok's straight-arm punches and jarring uppercuts sent sweat and blood flying from his adversary's head. By the time O'Riley managed to land a blow, he was weakened. Bill was easily landing five good punches for every one of O'Riley's clumsy ones.

Finally, the hulking Irishman collapsed to his knees, gave a mighty sigh, then sprawled on his face, unconscious.

Cheers went up from the workers who had witnessed this.

"Don't worry, fellow," Stratton called out to Bill. "We'll send a replacement over. And I'll have security haul O'Riley off the property. You handled that big galoot with real style, Mr. . . . ?"

"Lofley, Mr. Stratton," Wild Bill replied. "Ben Lofley. Just hired on yesterday as crew chief."

"And I can see why," Stratton praised. "Good work, Ben. I never much liked O'Riley."

"Thank you, Mr. Stratton."

Bill prepared to hop the next muck bucket. Despite Stratton's praise, however, Hickok could feel Earl Beckman's gaze studying him with silent speculation.

The rest of that first workday dragged on without further incident. However, toward the end of the shift, first word reached Deadwood of the robbery and killing of teamster Butch Winkler—

supposedly by Sioux warriors who had jumped the rez.

So Hickok took notice when Merrill Labun and Danny Stone didn't show up until late afternoon. Again it made him wonder: What did Owen McNulty know that got him killed?

Bill decided it was high time, on his first day off, to visit the Sioux at Copper Mountain.

Chapter Six

" 'Out West,' " Bill read aloud from Joshua's most recent dispatch, " 'you're just a face with a name. Nobody cares about your history. Unfortunately, that same apathy means nobody cares about your existence, either. On the American frontier, fewer things are cheaper than a man's life.' "

Hickok finished reading and looked up from the draft. It was Sunday morning, and both men were shoehorned into Bill's tiny room. Bill sat on the bed, Josh on the only chair.

"Well?" the young reporter demanded. "You told me I had to clear every story through you. I kept everything general and didn't mention anything to give us away. Is it all right to file it?"

Bill looked at the kid. "Sure, go ahead. It's damn good, kid. You write like I shoot—straight to the heart."

Bill handed the foolscap pages back to the youth and added, "But I'm worried, Longfellow."

"Why?"

"You might upstage me one of these days, you sneaky little runt! This is excellent scribbling. You're getting a name for yourself. Hell, I can't be sharing my women with you."

Both men laughed. Josh beamed proudly at this rare praise from his hero.

"Unless," Bill added, "you'd be willing to take Calamity Jane off my back?"

"Hunh! I wouldn't even be a snack for her." Josh shivered at the images his imagination conjured up. "You think," he added, serious now, "that she'll show up here?"

"Last I knew," Bill replied, "Jane was down in the old Spanish land-grant country, breaking in camels for the U.S. Cavalry. But I got a God-fear, kid, that she'll show up in Deadwood. If she ain't already here."

Bill stood up and picked up the scattergun he'd propped against the wall. He broke open the breech to make sure it was loaded. His Colt Peacemakers were still tucked out of sight in his saddlebag. Hickok missed wearing them as if he were separated from family.

"C'mon," he told Josh. "Elsie's got breakfast ready. Outside guests are welcome for two bits, so you can eat here. That woman sets out good grub. I swear, her biscuits're so light they need holding down."

"Will we have enough time to make it out to the Copper Mountain Reservation and back?" Josh asked. "If we don't show for work tomorrow, that'll ruin our cover."

"The rez is just a whoop and a holler from here," Bill assured him.

"Exactly how do the Sioux figure in?" Josh pressed as they took the stairs down.

"That one's got me treed," Bill admitted. "But I'll wager one thing. The big bosses at Harney's Hellhole don't really believe, for even one minute, that the Indians are heisting any gold ore."

"That's not what I'm hearing in the front office," Josh disagreed. "Beckman swears it's the Sioux."

Wild Bill gave the kid a pitying look. "They always talk who never think. You write like an angel sings—how can you be so consarn ignorant? If Indians were really stealing from white men, would Beckman just *bitch* about it?"

Josh mulled that as they approached the double doors leading into Elsie's dining room.

"Nah, you're right," the kid conceded. "There'd be Indian fever sweeping Deadwood six ways to Sunday."

"Damn straight. Those mining bosses would be howling crazy for Indian blood. But there hasn't been even one attack against the rez."

After a delicious breakfast of eggs, potatoes, biscuits, and side meat, the two men—using separate sides of the street—walked to the livery stable at the edge of town.

They found Lonnie Brubaker swamping out the stables.

"Hey up, Lonnie," Bill greeted the youth. "Our horses still alive, son?"

The half-wit kid grinned, revealing rabbit teeth. "They're just fine, Ben. You'll find 'em out in the paddock. Just like you asked, I ain't been stalling them nights."

"Good man."

Bill slipped a coin from his pocket and pressed it into the kid's hand. "Lonnie, do you know who Merrill Labun is when you see him?"

The kid nodded. Bill knew that no one could head west, out of town, without passing this spot.

"I need to know when he comes and goes. Can you write down numbers?"

The kid nodded again.

"Good. Each time he arrives in town, or leaves, just write it down, wouldja? Just write down the day and time."

Lonnie hesitated, perhaps unsure of Bill's motives.

"Lonnie," Bill confided, "I'm not a crook. I swear on my honor."

Lonnie searched Bill's eyes. Whatever he saw in them satisfied him. He nodded and took the coin. Bill and Josh grabbed their saddles and bridles and went out to the paddock to rig their mounts.

"Well groomed and well fed," Bill approved as his roan trotted over to nuzzle him in greeting.

"Bill?" Josh said while he centered his saddle. "Do you know anything about the Sioux at Copper Mountain."

"Not enough to brag about it," Bill admitted. He raised a stirrup out of his way and tightened the girth. "Pinkerton only knows the name of their leader, a subchief named Coyote Boy. Supposedly he palavers good English."

"We'll be trespassing if we go on the reservation, right?"

Bill stepped into a stirrup and vaulted into the saddle. "Yup," was all he said.

As the two men rode past the Lutheran church at the end of town, the sound of singing filled the street: "A Mighty Fortress Is Our God."

Josh still worried about their reception at the reservation.

"Well anyhow," he said out loud, "they can't have guns by law."

Bill snorted, then shook his head in amazement at the kid's faith in paper laws.

"Joshua, neither red man nor white has abided by a single treaty to the letter. There's guns, all right. But even if there ain't, if a Sioux wants to kill you, he's got many ways to do it without bullets. Matter of fact, a bullet would be merciful."

The Copper Mountain Indian Reservation comprised a few thousand acres of rolling scrubland no white men wanted. It lay fifteen miles southwest of Deadwood, connected by a good road established two decades earlier by the shortline stage between Deadwood and Lead.

The day was sunny, breezeless, and hot. Two horsebackers sent dust rising in brown swirls under their horses' hooves. The swirling plumes quickly crumbled to dust that powdered the roadside growth. Ragged tatters of cloud drifted across a sky as blue as a lagoon.

Now and then Bill took off his hat and whacked at flies with it. With his usual constant vigilance, he continuously scanned the surrounding terrain, watching for movements or reflections. Again Josh noticed how Bill had to squint close to see past the middle distances.

Finally they reached a fork in the trail. The right fork marked the beginning of the reservation. A sign in English declared this property off-limits to whites and instructed them to take the left fork.

"It could come any time now," Wild Bill told his companion as they bore right. "They've been watching us for a long time."

Josh was about to ask how Bill knew that. But almost the very moment they passed the warning sign, a series of yipping war cries made the hair on Josh's nape stand up.

At least a dozen well-armed, mounted braves suddenly descended from the tree cover and surrounded them. Josh stared at the angry, clay-colored Indians, his mouth dry with fright.

Bill, however, merely raised one arm high with the hand open—the universal sign for peace. He kept his face calm and impassive. Seeing him, Josh followed suit.

A warrior snatched the scattergun from its boot. Wild Bill ignored him.

"Which of you calls himself Coyote Boy?" Bill demanded in English.

A brave with perhaps thirty winters behind him rode forward. He wore doeskin leggings and a bone breastplate. His bridle was woven from buffalo hair, and his saddle was a sheepskin pad. Josh gaped at his big-bore German hunting rifle. The brave poked the muzzle into Bill's chest.

"I go by that name you said," he replied in excellent English. "But who said *you* may speak it aloud and steal my magic? You are nothing but a *wasichu* intruder. Which of us have you come to murder this time?"

"We have not come to kill," Bill assured him. "I do not kill the Lakota people. Ask about me at the council fires and the Spring Dance. I give life to the Lakota."

This foolish boast made Coyote Boy laugh out loud in scorn. He translated this for the others. They, too, howled in derisive scorn.

"And how," Coyote Boy demanded, "do you work this miracle, white-eyes?"

"You know of me," Bill assured him. "I am known to the Lakotas as the Ice Shaman."

For a moment Coyote Boy's stern face clearly looked startled. The Ice Shaman was the name Wild Bill Hickok had earned among Sioux down south in Nebraska. This was after he and an eccentric German inventor used a new invention, the ice-making machine, to save a dozen Sioux Indians dying of fever plague. They packed the sick in ice and thus brought their fevers down.

"*You* are the Ice Shaman?"

Coyote Boy's voice was skeptical. But Josh also noticed the hatred was gone.

Bill now played the ace up his sleeve—he produced the brightly dyed blue feather that Chief Yellow Bear had given him after saving his people.

This feather denoted that Hickok was a valued friend of the Lakota peoples.

No translation was needed once the feather came out. The braves all lowered their weapons. The warrior who took Bill's gun now handed it back.

"You are welcome here, Ice Shaman," Coyote Boy assured him. "You and your friend."

Everyone dismounted and retired to the temporary camp in a covert among the trees. A smiling, awestruck squaw served the famous hair-face and his companion strong white man's coffee laced with crude brown sugar.

"You have good English," Bill remarked to the subchief.

"I was sent to the mechanical arts school in Denver," Coyote Boy replied. He added scornfully, "They taught me how to salute the flag of my enemies. And to repair wagon wheels when we do not use wagons. I can also repair the furnaces we do not have. Why have you come to our remote home, Ice Shaman?"

Bill quickly explained that he was trying to get to the bottom of the "robberies" and killings taking place lately.

"Only a fool," Hickok concluded, "would believe that red men are stealing gold ore. Are you eating the ore wagons afterward?"

Coyote Boy translated and the people howled with mirth.

"I believe the white miners are taking it themselves. And I believe Owen McNulty"—here Bill politely made the cutoff sign for speaking of the dead—"found that out. That's why he was murdered."

Coyote Boy nodded. "As you say."

"I'm on your side," Bill assured him. "If this keeps up, the yellow legs will be sent to kill you."

At this reference to the cavalry, Coyote Boy spat with contempt. "Soldiers! Pah! Boys with their pants tucked into their boots."

"They are no Lakotas," Bill agreed. "Never could they win one-on-one with Indian fighters. But the hair-faces have the big-thundering guns. They will kill your women and children. We must end this trouble before your people do the Hurt Dance."

Coyote Boy saw the truth of all this. He nodded. "You speak solid words an Indian can place in his sash. What do you suggest, Ice Shaman?"

"I say teamwork will see us through," Hickok replied. "These miners, like white men everywhere, they are well organized. The time may come, and soon, when a battle with them will be necessary."

Coyote Boy only nodded, acknowledging the truth of this.

"Therefore," Bill continued, "I have come today to ask if you and your braves will join me when that time for battle arrives. There can be no victory without Lakota men to side me."

Coyote Boy said nothing at first. But pride was evident in his face, though he kept it stern as a warrior must.

"My people are doomed otherwise. It will be an honor to fight beside the savior of Chief Yellow Bear's people."

"Meantime," Bill advised, "lay low. Don't give the hair-faces cause to move against you. The worm will turn, Coyote Boy. We can win this battle if we use cunning and bravery."

Bill patted the walnut stock of his scattergun. "And a little well-aimed ammo," he added.

Chapter Seven

"Well, God kiss me," Wild Bill said out loud. "Look who's coming, junior."

Josh, still mulling their reception by the Sioux, focused his eyes ahead on the trail. A buggy with its top up against the dust approached from the direction of Deadwood.

The female driver wore a crisp white bonnet. But there was no mistaking the beautiful blond hair the color of ripe Kansas wheat.

The two riders cleared the trail to let the faro dealer pass, politely touching their hats as she drew near. Instead of rolling past, however, she reined in the big blood bay.

"Good day, gentlemen," she called out in a friendly tone. She gave them a quick and uncertain smile—a little bold, a little shy, a little sly. In that moment, Josh fell head over heels in love; Hickok, too was impressed. But his thoughts were a bit less sublime than the kid's.

She looked at Bill. "My name is Cassie Saint John. I'm not sure you remember me, Mister . . . ?"

"Lofley. Ben Lofley. Yes, ma'am, I do recall you from the Number 10."

Josh almost snorted at Bill's low-key response. *Recall?* Why, lord, a woman like her stood out, in that hole, like a sleek Yankee Clipper in a harbor of barges.

"Mr. Lofley," she said, "I noticed how you . . . handled that bully, Danny Stone. You seem like a very capable and confident man."

"Thank you, Miss Saint John."

"Nonetheless, I would like to offer a very friendly word of advice."

She paused, unsure.

"I'd welcome it, ma'am," Bill encouraged her. "I'm flattered, actually."

"Mr. Lofley, this bunch at Harney's Hellhole . . . well, let me just suggest that it might be wise to avoid antagonizing them. 'Accidents' tend to happen around here."

"Mining is dangerous work," Bill said, as if missing her drift.

"No. I mean accidents such as the one that killed my friend Owen McNulty."

"I heard that was murder, Miss Saint John, not an accident."

"My point exactly."

Bill touched his hat again. "I will indeed think

about your advice, ma'am. And I do thank you sincerely. I'm not one to seek trouble."

Josh watched a little glimmer of amused doubt spark in her green eyes. "I wonder about that, sir."

"I lost your drift there," Bill confessed. "Why would you wonder?"

"Mr. Lofley, I have this rare old photo in my room. It's a rather faded tintype of one James Butler Hickok."

She paused, and Bill did a great job—Josh thought—of maintaining a poker face.

"If I was Mr. Hickok," he suggested gallantly, "I'd be quite flattered to know you keep it. As it is, I confess I'm slightly jealous. We common men can hardly hope to compete with fame."

She smiled at his clever dissembling.

"What makes it rare," she pressed on, "is that it's one of the few known photographs where he's quite clean-cut."

Oh, man alive, Josh thought. *We're cooked.* This woman was Deke Stratton's concubine!

However, if anything, Hickok only played it even cooler.

"Is that a fact, Miss Saint John?"

"Yes. And compared to his usual hirsute style, he appears almost . . . stern and unbending. Still handsome, but less roguish. Your own face puts me in mind of that tintype."

" 'Preciate that, ma'am. No one's ever compared my face to a famous man. Why, you'll make me prideful and conceited."

Again that amused glimmer was back in her big, almond-shaped eyes.

"I think it's too late—you're already prideful and conceited, Mister . . . Lofley. Good day, gentlemen."

As her buggy clattered off, sending up dust plumes, Josh groaned.

"Aww, crimeny, Wild Bill! All our efforts shot to blazes. What do we do now?"

"Nothing," Bill replied calmly, clucking to his horse.

"Nothing? But she's close to Stratton."

" 'Close' is a loose word, kid. I know women—at least, her kind of woman. An ambitious female out here has no choice when she's on her own. Either she cottons up to the head hounds, or she gets bit. As long as I don't threaten her own plans, she'll live and let live. In fact . . ."

A little smile tugged at the corners of Bill's lips. "If she knows who I really am, she surely knows why I'm here. And just maybe she *wants* to see me succeed. That was no chance remark when she mentioned McNulty was her friend."

"She's sure pretty," Josh opined. He visualized her flawless mother-of-pearl skin.

"Mm," Bill agreed, his eyes scouring both sides of the trail. "Deadwood's only a few miles now. Kick your horse up to a canter, Longfellow. I want you and me to arrive separately."

Even before Josh could carry out the order, the sound of a high-power rifle cracked in the distance. It was not close enough to threaten them. But it startled both men into careful attention.

Several more shots boomed out—at least three

different guns, Wild Bill's trained ear quickly detected.

"Hunting rifles or target guns," he told Josh. "South of here. It's just sport shooters."

Josh's face regained some of its color. But as he pushed on ahead, Wild Bill called out: "Joshua?"

"Yeah?"

"Don't forget—around here, anyone can become part of the 'sport.' "

"That's holding and squeezing, Deke," Earl Beckman praised his friend. "You dropped it at three hundred yards!"

The sage grouse Stratton had just shot flumped to the ground.

"You want the bird, Mr. Stratton?" called back a half-breed kid who was out ahead of them, beating the bushes for game.

"Leave it for the turkey vultures, Tommy," Stratton replied. "Go on ahead and see if you can scare up some four-legged game."

The youth moved obediently forward. Stratton, Keith Morgan, and Earl Beckman followed at a leisurely pace, rifles muzzle down. Cassie Saint John had just joined them in a huge, brush-filled meadow adjacent to Stratton's horse-breeding ranch. She carried a pongee parasol against the brutal rays of the sun.

"You know, Earl," Deke remarked casually as he thumbed cartridges into the ammo well of a silver-trimmed Swiss Vetterli rifle. "This new crew chief, Ben Lofley—he whaled the tar out of O'Riley. I never saw any man stand up to that big mick bully.

Lofley's got sand. He could be useful to you in security."

"He's got sand, all right," Beckman agreed. "But I'm not quite as sanguine about him as you are, Deke. The man's a blank slate."

"Most men are, out West."

Earl said nothing to this, at first, only looking around at Deke's spread as if appraising its value.

Besides this 20,000-acre breeding ranch, Stratton owned a magnificent estate in Virginia's hunt country as well as his own private island in the Gulf of Mexico. Financially speaking, he considered himself a forward-oriented man, if not quite a visionary. Thus, he'd even begun speculating heavily in European art masterpieces. Art was a prime investment because the real stuff could only gain in value.

Finally Earl decided to reply.

"Yes, most men are blank slates out here. But 'most men' can't whip Brennan O'Riley."

Stratton considered Beckman's remark and frowned, deciding the man was being coy with him again. Deke did not disdain subtlety in a man—but he never let it slow him down, either.

"You want to spell that out plain, Earl?"

"All right, I will. When I was in the war, I learned to read men's eyes. A gunman—a true gunman who lives and dies by gun law—has a different look from other men."

Cassie, who appeared to be occupied in picking a bouquet of wildflowers, was in fact hanging on to every word.

"And you're implying that Ben Lofley has that 'look'?"

Beckman nodded.

"Not implying. I'm giving it to you plain with the bark still on it. He's a hardened killer. Harder, in his way, than any man on your payroll. Myself and Merrill included."

Stratton mulled this, his thin lips pressed in a grim frown. He wasn't convinced. Still, it all made perfect sense.

After all, as he himself knew, the job of power was to disguise true motives with deceptive rhetoric. Thus it was that a small, elite group of powerful men ran the world. Their private lives were completely unlike what the rabble imagined. Through fraud and illusion and comfortable lies, the masses could be controlled. So why couldn't a clever killer employ the same tricks on the power brokers?

"More smokestacks and businessmen," Deke finally said. "That's what the American West needs. Not these strutting-peacock gunmen romanticized in dime novels."

"Ho!" Keith Morgan shouted. "Lookit, boss!"

Tommy's efforts in beating the bushes with a boat oar had suddenly produced a prize: A tawny bobcat was startled out from hiding. It tore off across the huge clearing, bearing for a woods about two hundred yards off.

Stratton lifted the butt plate of the rifle into his shoulder socket, drew a quick offhand bead, and squeezed off a round. The bobcat leaped straight up, somersaulted in midair, and landed dead in the parched grass, hind legs twitching a few times.

Tommy pulled a curved skinning knife from his sash, ready to take the animal's pelt.

"Just leave it, Tommy," Stratton shouted. "I'm in a hurry today. We're heading back to the house."

Cassie spoke up.

"Don't you even want the hide? Or is it just the killing you three crave?"

"Just the killing," Morgan said bluntly—he despised Cassie almost as much as she despised him.

Deke, however, contradicted this remark.

"It's not the kill we're proud of, sweet love. It's the kill that proves a man's good *aim*. These animals are just moving targets."

"That's right," Beckman concurred. "Targets that move even faster than humans."

Chapter Eight

Like the miners, the clerks employed by Harney's Hellhole were required to be on the job shortly after sunrise. But supervision was more lax, and less brutal, among the "paper collars," as the laboring men called them with contempt. And perhaps a little envy, too. These weak but learned men were treated with some visible signs of respect from the company.

"Mr. Mumford," called out the head clerk, and Joshua immediately became politely attentive.

"Yes, Mr. Baxter?"

Supervisor Stanley Baxter was assigning jobs for the morning work stint. He was small and slightly bowed, yet radiated an Episcopalian gravity that lent him authority.

"Mr. Mumford, the mailbag came in last night from Rapid City. Eventually, you are to answer any letters from our French or German partners."

Baxter paused to push his bifocals up higher on his nose. He studied Josh intently across the big room. "But as usual, you must first submit English translations of these letters to Mr. Beckman's office."

"Yessir."

"You will then be supplied with responses, in English, from Mr. Beckman. You will carefully translate those responses into French or German and send the replies overseas. Understood?"

"Yessir. Clearly."

Josh had not yet translated any important or urgent letters. But he had studied copies of some on file. The overseas investors were naturally deeply concerned about profit losses from the recent robberies of ore wagons. What Josh knew, and even Deke Stratton did not, was that these same foreign investors had secretly employed Pinkerton's Agency.

Baxter droned on, parcelling out work for about a dozen clerks and copiers. They occupied one wing of the sprawling framework structure. A few of the clerks were discreetly eating bear-sign, the local name for doughnuts.

By claiming a slight nearsightedness, Josh had landed a desk near the inner wall with its bracket-mounted lamps. This was crucial because the adjoining room was Earl Beckman's private office. And only a cheap flockboard wall separated it from Josh.

For the next two hours Josh labored at translating a long letter from Berlin. He was forced to constantly consult a dictionary, and several times he could only guess at the proper verb tenses. However, it was only routine correspondence about financial and accounting matters.

Josh found his task difficult because his thoughts kept drifting to Cassie Saint John. Not just her spun-gold hair and ocean-green eyes. But also to the danger she now represented. She knew that Ben Lofley was really Wild Bill Hickok!

Bill, however, seemed to find that fact amusing. Almost as if it were a game between him and Cassie. And with that thought came another: That's *exactly* what it was—a seduction game and both Cassie and Bill were willing players.

That's just like Hickok, Josh realized. For him, sex and danger went hand-in-hand: the kill and the conquest. It was as if, for Hickok and a certain rare kind of woman, the normal rules of courtship were far too tame.

Josh's thoughts were rudely interrupted by a boom-cracking explosion that rocked the entire building. But no one showed much reaction—it was only another of Keith Morgan's powerful underground demolitions, opening up a new stope.

About an hour before the first break, Josh heard someone knock loudly on Beckman's door. He was bid enter.

Moving inconspicuously, Josh leaned right as if merely shifting his position on the chair. But now his ear was pressed against the thin flockboard wall.

*   *   *

"Come in, Merrill, come in," Earl Beckman called out in his polished tones soft as southern magnolias. "How'd the blast go this morning?"

Labun closed the door with his heel. Then he eased his huge bulk into a chair.

"Deke's got him a grin from ear to ear. Says it exposed a whole new lode of rich ore."

Beckman, too, smiled to show his satisfaction. He steepled his fingers together and rested his chin on them. Despite his elation, however, a frown soon ousted the smile.

"I have a couple of reasons for calling you in," he told Labun. "One is to remind you about this new crew chief, Ben Lofley."

"You still worried he's a Pinkerton, boss?"

Beckman's fox-terrier face sharpened even more in concentration.

"If he is," the security chief conceded, "he's not the usual caliber of Pinkerton man. What do you think? You see more of him than I do."

Labun considered the question, picking at his teeth with a match.

"He don't size up like no Pinkerton to me neither," he finally replied. "Still . . . there's something about him that won't tally."

"My point precisely. Deke doesn't see that so clearly as we do, and it worries me. Now, the second reason I called you in, Merrill, is that other matter we spoke of."

"What other matter would that be, boss?"

"Do you remember our little discussion about the Indian lovers in Congress?" Beckman prompted his minion.

"You mean—how they're starting to scream blue murder? Stuff about how ridiculous it is to claim Indians would steal gold ore?"

"Exactly."

Merrill nodded. "When you want it done?"

"As soon as possible. In fact, tonight would be excellent."

"Oh yeah? Why's that?"

"The Rapid City Express will be transporting some . . . prominent folks from Boston."

Labun nodded, then hove his weight out of the chair. "Then tonight it is, boss."

The popular stagecoach route between Rapid City and Casper originated in the rugged Black Hills. But after a slow, often uncomfortable two-day start, the coach fairly flew across the flat, open terrain of Wyoming's Thunder Basin.

There had been no serious Indian trouble along this route since the 1860s—and the crackdown by the U.S. Cavalry after Custer's Seventh was massacred. Now only the Apaches under Geronimo still ran free, and they were way down south in the Dragoon Mountains.

During the quarter of the full moon, the Rapid City Express traveled day and night, stopping only at designated stage-relay stations to change teams and grease the axles.

"Cheyenne Crossing's coming up soon," Ned Pollard called over to his shotgun rider, a young newcomer named Andy Hanchon. "That's our last stop in the hill country. Come dawn, we'll be hauling ass across the flats. *Haw* there, you four-legged devils, *haw!*"

Ned reined in hard and pulled back mightily on the brake handle. The wildly rocking Concord coach slowed for a sharp elbow bend at the bottom of the mountain slope.

"Sir!" protested a sharp, cultured female voice from a window behind and below the two men. "*Must* you drive so recklessly? My husband has . . . regurgitated his supper all over us!"

Ned Pollard slapped a fat thigh. His right elbow dug into Andy's ribs.

"You hear that, Andy? That fat preacher from Boston *regurgitated* his supper all over his blue-nosed, horse-faced wife and them soft-mouthed missionaries. Re-goddamn-gurgitated? Well, that caps the climax, mister!"

"Sorry, ma'am!" he barely managed to shout. "Got to keep the schedule!"

Both men hooted in mirth under a placid, moonlit sky alive with glittering stars. Ned was stout, middle-aged, a bit hound-doggy in the jowls. Half his age, Andy was dark and lean. A Winchester repeater lay across his thighs.

The Concord, rocking on its leather braces, careened through the sharp turn. Someone thumped on the roof of the coach in protest. Ned laughed like a hyena as he cracked his whip over the team, urging them to go faster.

To hell with that soul saver! If they hurried, Ned knew they'd all be just in time for hot biscuits, bacon, and beans at Cheyenne Crossing.

"My God, sir, take pity!" groaned the high-pitched masculine voice of the preacher. "I shall surely die in this infernal contraption!"

"Go ahead and croak," Ned joked, knowing only Andy could hear him. "Leaves more eats for me."

Thwap!

The arrow point embedded deep in the box only inches from Ned's hip. In that generous moonlight he could see the shaft quiver as it spent its deadly force.

A painful cry rose from Andy's side of the box. Ned, fear hammering in his temples, glanced right and felt his gorge rise: Andy was still alive, but arrows protruded from him like quills! Two in his right thigh, two more in his upper right arm, one high on his back.

Even as Ned laid into the lash, an ear-piercing scream rose from the interior of the coach.

"Oh, good heart of God! Roger! Oh, Roger, Esther's been hit with an arrow!" shouted a female voice, almost drowned out by the wounded woman's repeated screams of terror and pain.

"My *eye!*" Esther cried out in a feral, hysterical voice. "Oh no, dear Lord no, not my *eye!*"

Indians? Ned asked himself, a puzzled numbness flowing through him as he drove the team to a reckless pace along the sloping trail. So all the crazy rumors weren't so crazy, after all? The Copper Mountain Sioux had jumped the rez and greased their faces for war? Holy Hannah!

He could hear the unmistakable sound of their yipping war cries though Ned couldn't actually see any of them. Injun trouble this late in the game . . .

At least the attack seemed to be over—no more flint-tipped arrows pelted them.

"You just hold on, Andy," he told the pitifully groaning youth. "I know it hurts, son, but you know we dar'n't stop. There's a doctor in Buckhorn."

Ned shouted this same news to the passengers, advising them they dare not stop yet. The only response from the coach was Esther's horrible cries of pain, terrible and almost inhuman in their despair.

Wild Bill knew, damn good and well, there'd be trouble tonight if he visited the Number 10. But he figured he was in Deadwood to lance a tumor, not to treat it.

It was well after dark by the time he arrived, fresh off a good feed of corn pone and back ribs at Elsie's. The place was lively as a bordertown bordello. Stratton, Morgan, and Beckman occupied their usual table in the back. But at least there was no sign yet of Merrill Labun or Danny Stone.

Those two, Bill reminded himself, tend to come and go at odd hours.

Bill found an open spot at the far end of the curving bar. The barkeep in the gray Stetson, Jim Bob Lavoy, kept his face averted when Hickok ordered. Lavoy banged a schooner of foaming beer down, scooped up Bill's nickel, and moved on with a gruff " 'preciate it."

Bill liked a cold beer now and then. But his usual habit was to nurse a bottle of Old Taylor. However, he dare not live beyond his means as

Ben Lofley. Old Taylor ran almost six bits a bottle.

Even as he mulled all this, Hickok could feel Cassie Saint John watching him. His eyes found hers in the mirror.

She smiled and then openly waved, ignoring the ring of clamoring bettors surrounding the faro table.

Bill gave the slightest of nods to acknowledge her greeting. A moment later Lonnie Brubaker tugged at Bill's sleeve.

"Mr. Lofley? I got a message for you from your friend Charlie Mumford."

"Written or spoken?"

"Uhh, spoken, sir."

"Say it low, Lonnie, just for me."

"Yessir. The message is this: Labun met with his boss. Something will happen tonight."

Bill nodded. "Thank you, son. Labun leave town tonight?"

"Yessir. About six o'clock."

"He back yet?"

"Nuh-unh. Leastways, not so's I know."

"Good man. Here, get a sarsaparilla to take with you."

"*Thanks*, Mister Lofley."

The kid bought a soda pop and threaded his way toward the batwings. Bill flicked his eyes toward the mirror again to watch Cassie.

She and the case-tender were evidently on break. As usual, she rose to join Deke Stratton at his table. But before she did, Bill watched her snap open a little alligator jewel case.

Cassie removed a gold quarter-eagle and

handed it to the case-tender. She said something to him. He nodded and relayed both message and money to Jim Bob Lavoy.

A moment later the barkeep thumped a pony glass and a signed bottle of Old Taylor onto the deal counter in front of Hickok.

"Compliments of the faro dealer," Lavoy said in a surly tone, his face still averted. He was gone before a surprised Bill could even say thanks.

He stared at the bottle, realizing that Cassie Saint John had just upped the ante in their little seduction game. By now there could be no more doubt of it—she *knew* the quiet laborer was in fact legendary killer Wild Bill Hickok.

Bill turned away from the bar and bowed in her direction—a gesture not wasted on Deke Stratton. But Hickok was glad Stratton noticed. He *wanted* to stand out as a cut or two above the common man. Bill's goal was to make Stratton decide he needed this new man.

But Hickok's moment of glory appeared to be short-lived—even as Cassie settled between Stratton and Beckman, the batwings banged open. Merrill Labun and Danny Stone stood there side by side, their eyes seeking trouble.

Here comes the fandango, Bill told himself as he knocked back his first swallow of bourbon. I'm damned if I'll break this bottle over their heads, Bill thought as he pushed his whiskey to a safer spot.

In the mirror, Hickok watched the two new arrivals approach him. Everyone at Stratton's table watched, too. But nobody, Bill told himself, is watching closer than Jim Bob Lavoy.

"Lookit this son of a bitch," Stone's nasal voice carped beside him. "Swaggering it around like a big man, drinking top-shelf liquor. Ain't *you* the big toff, Lofley?"

Bill flicked his cold gaze to the loudmouth, then to Labun. The latter was taking no sides in this confrontation. Stone's bandage, Bill noticed, was smudged with dirt.

"Merrill, I thought you said this jasper doesn't hold a grudge?" Bill remarked.

"Oh, ain't he the funny bunny?" Stone jeered. "I say your mother's a whore Lofley, know that?"

"My sister's better," Hickok replied calmly. Several men nearby laughed. This only further enraged Stone.

"It's past talk, you white-livered bastard! I'm bracing you."

"I'm not armed," Bill said truthfully.

"That won't work, jelly guts, on account I got you a gun right here."

Besides the long-barreled Walker Colt in his tied-down holster, Stone had a .44 shoved into the waist of his trousers.

"Here, take this and—"

Stone never finished that sentence or any other. The very moment the .44 cleared his belt, a pistol spoke its piece. Merrill Labun swore in shock and disgust when Stone's bloody brains sprayed one cheek.

The big man collapsed, a corpse even before he—it—hit the floor. The barroom went so silent the tinkle of the player piano seemed like a roar.

Lavoy stood behind the bar, his pistol still smoking.

"You goddamn fool!" Labun managed. "You just murdered a man in cold blood!"

"He's the fool, you big-mouthed lout. From where I stand, that peckerwood just drew steel on an unarmed man. Any pea-brained idjit will tell you you *never* clear leather in a crowded barroom."

"He's right," Earl Beckman affirmed. "By frontier tradition, recognized in court, the only justification for drawing a weapon in a saloon is self-defense. Jim Bob was in the right."

"Good thing for you, Mr. Lofley," Deke Stratton added, "that our bartender seems to like you."

Deke paused and glanced at the bottle of Old Taylor, then at Cassie. "As do others," he concluded.

By now Hickok had guessed the truth about who Jim Bob Lavoy really was. And he was damned if having a lovestruck Calamity Jane on his trail was a "good thing." Sure, she had saved his bacon a few times in the past. But something about that man-hungry female made Bill prefer to face down a blazing six-gun.

Labun was still outraged. Stratton and Beckman had returned to their table, dismissing the incident. The saloon returned to its normal controlled chaos as two Chinese workers began dragging the body outside—more money for the undertaker.

"You ain't heard the last of this," Labun threatened the bar dog.

"Then you ain't heard the last of *this*," Jane assured him, as fearless as a rifle. She wagged the pistol at him before she dropped it back into its holster.

"Go ask a *real* marshal, you tin star," she added. Her eyes finally met Bill's directly. "Ask somebody like Tom Smith or Red Dog Malone or maybe even Wild Bill Hickok himself. They'll all tell you I was in the right."

"Wild Bill Hickok can kiss my ass," Labun retorted.

Jane chuckled, for Wild Bill was in fact close enough to do just that.

"He sure could," she agreed, still goading Bill with her eyes. "But I doubt he'll ever do that, Merrill. More likely, he'll just free your soul for you."

Chapter Nine

"One thing's for sure," Joshua goaded Wild Bill. "With Jane working at the Number 10, you'd best be discreet with that pretty faro dealer. Jane figures *you* complete her destiny. She's only keeping you alive until you figure that out."

"It ain't just her jealousy I got to fret," Bill corrected him. "What I'm worried about most is Jane getting drunk. Christ, you've seen her, kid. You saw it tonight. She knocks back a few quarts of Doyle's Hop Bitters, and she gets those crazy impulses to start shooting whatever moves. That's why she's blacklisted from every bar west of the Mississippi."

The two men shared Elsie Nearhood's kitchen all to themselves. Elsie had gone to bed. The rest of the boarders had either turned in or were still out in town raising hell.

Hickok had heated up the huge pot of coffee Elsie always left on the stove. Now he and Josh were working on their second cup—they still had a long night ahead of them.

"Jane can be useful at times," Bill conceded, both hands wrapped round the pottery mug. "But she's like lit dynamite, and you don't know when she might go off. I *want* to stand out in Stratton's mind, sure. That's how a man gets noticed. But the wrong kind of attention will just get me killed."

Bill said all this matter-of-factly, as if quoting beef prices. He drained his coffee mug and set it on the sideboard.

"That cowboy coffee should keep us sassy for a few more hours. C'mon, kid, let's get our horses."

"Where we riding to?" Josh demanded as he followed Bill into the foyer.

"Hold it down, you'll wake everybody up. We're taking a little ride out to Stratton's breeding ranch."

A feather of fear tickled the bumps of Joshua's spine. "Man alive! But why?"

They were in the street now, enveloped in shadows. Bill looked carefully all around them before he answered.

"I want to cut some sign, that's why. I've got this little theory about those 'Indians' that attacked the Rapid City Express."

"What theory is that?" Josh pressed. But he had learned by now that Hickok answered questions in his own good time. Sure enough, Bill ignored him.

Ore wagons still rumbled through the streets,

lanterns hanging out from the lead team's yoke on long metal arms. But the two men were nearly invisible on the rammed-dirt sidewalk. They reached the livery and found Lonnie curled up asleep in one of the stalls.

Bill reluctantly shook the kid awake.

"Sorry to disturb you, son. Just one question: How do I get to Deke Stratton's spread?"

The kid muttered directions, then nodded off again. Wild Bill and Josh grabbed their riding rigs and went out into the moonlit paddock. Their horses seemed to welcome the prospect of exercise—both animals readily submitted to the bit.

The two riders left Deadwood at a trot, bearing southwest toward Lead.

"Could just be happenchance," Hickok remarked. "But this same route eventually takes you to Cheyenne Crossing—that's near where the express was attacked."

Moonlight was generous in a starlit sky. They heard little besides the clopping of their horses' hooves and the steady crackle of insects. The rolling landscape surrounding them was scarred deep by erosion gullies.

After a long climb they pulled in to let their horses blow. Only now did Hickok open a saddlebag to retrieve his ivory-grip Peacemakers. He strapped the gunbelt on and adjusted it low on his hips. Josh watched him slide a box of .44 rimfires into his shirt pocket.

They hit the trail again. Just north of Lead, Bill pointed out the marker Lonnie had mentioned—

an Indian cairn that rose about fifteen feet into the air.

They veered at right angles from the main trail, following the private lane to Stratton's Double-S spread. Soon Josh could see horses grazing in a big, grassy draw on their left.

"Hold it," Bill told him. "This will be far enough for checking my theory."

Both men swung down and quickly hobbled their mounts. Then Bill squatted on his ankles and studied the ground for some time. Josh had seen him read sign like this before—an impressive skill that hinted at Hickok's earlier life on a dangerous frontier.

"Yup," Bill announced after about two minutes of ghostly silence.

He stood up again, working the kink out of his back.

"This is where the so-called Regulators rendezvoused before attacking," he told Josh. "I count fresh tracks for at least a dozen men. They all rode in about the same time, all on iron-shod horses."

The wind gusted, pressing the grass flat, and Bill paused to listen. Both hands rested on the butts of his Colts.

"Then you can see," Bill went on, "where the same number of riders left on unshod horses. Different animals, smaller—Indian scrubs. Providing that many animals is a cinch on a horse ranch. This wouldn't hang a man in a court of law, but it proves my hunch."

"But why would Deke Stratton want to attack a bunch of missionaries?" Josh wondered.

"He doesn't. The target was intended to make headlines. Headlines about Indian trouble in the Black Hills."

"Yeah," Josh said, "I get it now. That supports his crazy claims about Sioux stealing ore wagons. And those newspaper stories will back him in court. He can also send them overseas to his partners."

"*Now* you're thinking like a criminal," Wild Bill praised him. "C'mon, let's vamoose. Sunup comes mighty early when you're a working stiff."

Even as Bill fell silent, both men heard it: the fast drumbeat of riders approaching from the direction of the ranch.

"Move quick!" Hickok snapped. "We can still get to cover before they spot us."

Both men quickly untied the rawhide hobbles. Hickok vaulted into the saddle, wheeled his roan around, then waited for Josh.

Unfortunately, Joshua had forgotten a valuable lesson that Hickok had repeated to him several times: When you leave your horse with the girth loose, you always place a stirrup on the saddle horn as a reminder.

The moment Josh stepped into the stirrup, his loose saddle slid around and dumped the kid in the dust. And now the riders were so close Hickok could make them out in the buttery moonlight.

"Who goes there?" one of them shouted. "Give the pass!"

Bill cursed as Joshua scrambled to his feet and began resetting his saddle. "Any old damn day now, sweetheart!"

Bill spotted five, no, six riders, all abreast. Maybe some of the Regulators or perhaps Stratton's ranch hands. Whoever they were, they weren't likely law-abiding citizens.

A rifle spoke its piece, and Bill heard the bullet hum by. Now several of the men were shooting, and the horses were starting to spook.

"Well, God kiss me!"

Bill cursed at his bad luck—fancy shooting would announce the presence of Wild Bill Hickok like a calling card. But he had no choice now thanks to Josh's greenhorn idiocy.

Bill drew his right-hand gun and did something he hated doing—he shot the horses, all six of them. He simply had no alternative. He dare not kill possibly innocent men. After all, he and the kid *were* trespassing, so these men had every right to shoot.

Bill's stunning display of marksmanship shocked the men into passivity. They merely crouched behind their downed animals, afraid to shoot back—their muzzle flashes would give this ace shooter easy targets.

"Are you finally ready, young lady?" Bill said sarcastically when Josh mounted his lineback.

Their horses had been craving a good run. Now they got one as the two men returned to Deadwood.

They made it back to town without further incident. But now Bill was worried. Whoever those men were, it wouldn't take them long to noise it about: There was a dead-aim gunsel somewhere around Deadwood. A man able to drop six horses, in the dark at rifle range, with six shots from a short gun.

Despite the late hour, both men curried the sweat from their horses and rubbed them down good before turning them out into the paddock.

"Still got time for about three hours' sleep," Wild Bill remarked as they left the darkened livery stable.

"Sorry I botched it tonight," Josh said.

"So am I, kid. I've never met a horse yet that deserved to be killed. Wish now I'd just shot the riders."

Josh frowned, dejected at letting his hero down. Hickok threw an arm around the reporter's bony shoulders.

"Buck up, Longfellow. For a jasper raised in Philadelphia, you'll do to take along."

The two men parted in the shadows beside Elsie Nearhood's boarding house. Hickok climbed the narrow back steps to his tiny room and dropped the bar across the door. Then he fell into bed wearing everything but his boots.

Bill fell into a deep, dreamless sleep until the shrill steam whistle blasted him awake at dawn. He woke up feeling good—three hours of uninterrupted sleep was a bounty for Wild Bill.

Still, as he trudged up the slope toward Harney's Hellhole, a feeling of expectation tickled Bill's scalp.

Today something important would happen. And Hickok knew he had to be ready when it did.

* * *

"Lofley!"

For three straight hours Hickok had been hard at it, sorting ore from muck and tossing it out of swaying slusher buckets. The monotonous, repetitive labor tended to put a man into a trance.

"Lofley!"

The voice finally slapped Bill back to the present. One of Beckman's security men trotted beside Bill's bucket.

"What?"

The guard hooked a thumb up toward the complex of offices on a far slope.

"Mr. Stratton wants to talk to you. His private office is that building that sits off by itself, above the others."

Bill nodded and finished his bucket. Just before it reached the edge of the pit he jumped out. He told Taffy he was temporarily in charge. Then Bill headed toward the offices, wiping his filthy hands on his Levis.

Did Stratton know who he was? Cassie might have told him. Or maybe that equestrian slaughterfest last night, at Stratton's ranch, had tipped Bill's hand. If so, Hickok knew he might be walking into a trap.

But refusing to go was not an option. Bill decided to hide behind his best poker face and just play it hand by hand.

Halfway to Stratton's office, Bill had to pass through the squalid housing area. Women old before their time hung stained laundry out in the hot sun while little shirttail brats clung to their skirts. Men who worked the night shift, loading ore, gathered in groups to drink beer, pitch horse-shoes, arm wrestle, or bet on footraces between the children—anything to alleviate the boredom of a miner's life.

Bill also noticed several armed guards around the powder magazine. Miners were a disgruntled bunch of workers, capable of violent riots at any moment. That posed problems for big mining operations, which kept plenty of dynamite and nitro-glycerine on hand. Also kegs of black powder for shaped charges.

All that destructive power, Bill mused, and it's in the hands of Keith "Boomer" Morgan. The pride of the Confederate Army. Immortalized in one Union ballad as "the Grim Reaper in Gray." The man should have been hanged for war crimes; instead, he was a mine captain sharing the good life with Deke Stratton.

By now Hickok had reached the last building on the sprawling lot, Stratton's private office. Two more hard-eyed security men stood guard out front. But they greeted Hickok with some defer-ence—why? he wondered. Unless they had orders from Stratton to do so?

The door stood propped open with a chunk of ore. Stratton saw Hickok approaching.

"Come on in, Ben!" he called out affably, even rising from behind his neat desk to shake Hickok's hand, dirt and all. "Take a load off, working man."

Bill slacked into a chair at the corner of the desk. The office was pleasant, but hardly pom-pous. There was the usual American flag, of course. And a huge map on the back wall showed every shaft or stope that had been blasted into the mountain.

Stratton picked up a copy of the *Rapid City Register* from his desk. He read out loud for the new arrival's benefit:

" 'The victim, Mrs. Esther Emmerick, was a Methodist missionary from Indiana who came west to teach the savages how to speak and write English. Evidently, the same arrow that pierced her eye also penetrated the skull, lacerating the brain. She died of internal hemorrhaging in the cranium.' "

Stratton fell silent and slapped the newspaper back down onto his desk.

"Tell me, Ben," he said pleasantly. "How do you feel about this unfortunate incident?"

Bill shrugged. "It's a damn shame for the lady, Mr. Stratton. But it's none of my mix. I'm not one to worry unduly over what doesn't concern me."

Stratton smiled at Bill's candor. Most men would have made rhetorical statements of outrage.

"I've been watching you, Ben. And I like what I see. To quote an old trailsman, you're one of those rare men whom bees refuse to sting. Men like you shouldn't be lugging lunch pails."

Hickok returned the smile. "Now you mention it, I don't recall ever being stung by a bee. Wasp nor hornet, neither. But I have been snakebit."

Both men laughed.

"Hell, even Cassie likes you, Ben, and she's not easy to please. Tell me—did you grow up poor?" Stratton demanded bluntly.

"Poor as Job's turkey, boss."

"So did I, Ben. Christ, my people were dirt-poor. My old man topped sugar beets in Colorado right alongside Mexicans."

Stratton rose, crossed to the open front door, and pulled it shut. He returned to his desk and sat down. He spoke in a lower vice.

"Ben, between me and my . . . closest associates, there are no complicated arrangements. And very little that's put down on paper. Just a sort of . . . *subrosa* accord. Do you know what that means?"

"A sort of unwritten agreement, right?"

Stratton beamed. "Exactly. And *loyalty* is at the heart of this unwritten agreement. Loyalty is just as essential in business as in war, don't you think, Ben?"

Wild Bill Hickok was notorious for being a one-man outfit, loyal to nothing but the harsh code of gun law. Thus, the lie came easily.

"To me, that's not even debatable," he told Stratton. "Even a simple cowboy will fight for the brand of his employer. Even if he hates the man personally."

Clearly Deke could not have wished for a better answer.

"So *that's* where you got that steel in your eyes," he said enthusiastically. "Range wars, right?"

Bill nodded, and this time it was no lie. He had in fact ended the bloody Kinkaid County War in Wyoming only a year earlier.

"Tell me, Ben . . . what's your opinion of Earl Beckman? Frankly now."

Hickok knew, of course, that he was being tested. However, the exact nature of the test was Stratton's secret. But Bill knew he couldn't penetrate to the heart of the Regulators without taking risks.

"Well, since you ask, Mr. Stratton, I don't trust him."

Stratton's behavior now made Bill wish he could laugh outright. Like many pompous men of wealth, Stratton usually feigned a benign indifference to men who lacked money. But he seemed keenly interested in Bill's insights on Beckman.

"Why?" Stratton pressed. "*Why* don't you trust him?"

This, Hickok realized, was the moment he had sworn to be ready for. God guide his tongue . . . He wanted Stratton to perceive him as a simple man with sound instincts.

"No special reason, Mr. Stratton. But that man is tricky—tricky as a redheaded woman. And loyal only to himself."

Stratton nodded, obviously satisfied with this opinion. Even pleased.

"Between me and you, Ben, I'm a little worried about having Earl in charge of security. I confess I have his desk searched regularly. The man has a certain penchant for . . . accumulating documents. Documents he really has no business keeping in his desk. Never the originals, of course. Copies. Why is he bothering to do that?"

Stratton didn't need to elaborate. Men in Beckman's job often worried about future legal actions.

He was either covering his own ass or preparing to nail someone else's.

"I have a theory about men like Earl," Stratton mused, perhaps thinking out loud. "Men who live and breathe for the rebel cause even today, almost ten years after the war. I believe their fanaticism makes them loyal *only* to that lost cause."

Stratton seemed to recall himself. He gave Hickok a perfunctory smile.

"Ben, I'm glad we had this little confab. Keep it close to your vest, eh? I still need time to . . . evaluate this matter. Meantime, I'd appreciate you keeping your eyes open wide, if you take my meaning?"

Bill nodded as he stood up, preparing to leave. Deke slid a pigskin wallet from the inner pocket of his jacket. He handed his employee several new banknotes. One of them, Bill noticed, was a twenty.

"There may be some changes around here," Stratton added. "If so, I've already got you in mind, Ben, for a hefty promotion. We'll be in touch, all right?"

Hickok kept the triumph out of his eyes. "You bet, Mr. Stratton," was all he said before he left.

Chapter Ten

After almost two weeks on the job, Hickok and Joshua had become regulars at the Number 10. Clerks stood out at night in their clean corduroy pants and low broughams. But it was safe to meet there at lunchtime, when miners and clerks often commingled for the lunch specials.

"So now we know that Stratton doesn't trust Beckman," Josh said thoughtfully when Bill had summed up this morning's meeting with Stratton.

"Do we?" Hickok challenged. "That's what he says, ain't it?"

This suggestion made Josh frown. "You mean . . . you think it's a trap?"

"I don't think so, no. But why the hell not? What better bait if Deke thinks I might be a Pinkerton op?"

"So what do we do?"

Bill stuck a skinny Mexican cigar between his teeth and scratched a phosphor across the scarred table. Intimidated by Calamity Jane's proximity at the bar, Hickok had insisted on a table.

"We can't hedge now," Bill admitted between puffs. As usual under pressure, he resorted to gambling metaphors. "The longer we let them bluff, the more danger we lose our entire stake. I say we take Deke's hand at face value. I think he really *is* watching Beckman like a cat on a rat."

Joshua forked steaming Hungarian goulash into his mouth. Like all the food out West, it was too damn salty. He repeated his question. "So what do we do?"

"What we always do, kid—we shake things up a little and see what falls out."

To any onlookers, Bill merely appeared to be reaching for a hunk of bread. But as his hand passed Josh's plate, the reporter heard something clunk onto the table.

Josh's eyebrows almost touched in puzzlement. He stared at the queerest-looking skeleton key he'd ever seen. Instead of one bit at the end of the shaft, there were three.

"What's that?" he demanded.

"Put it in your pocket before somebody sees it. That's the lad, and *keep* it hidden, hear? Don't let the other clerks see it. It's called a bar key, and it's illegal to possess one. Matter of fact, in most states it's five years at hard labor if you're caught with one."

Josh paled and quit eating. "Man alive! And it's in *my* pocket?"

"Easy, kid. If all goes well, you'll have it less than a day. See, the bar key is the primary tool of cracksmen back East in the big cities. Burglars who specialize in picking locks to gain entry. Locks, especially out here on the frontier, generally fit one of a few simple types."

"Cracksmen?" Josh repeated. "You mean me? I have to—"

"No, you young fool, *us*. You'll do the entry part while I take care of the guards."

"Enter what?"

"Deke Stratton's office," Bill replied calmly.

Joshua, the son of a pious Quaker mother and an honest judge father, rarely swore. He did now, making Hickok grin.

"Jesus Katy Christ, Bill! Stratton's office? What is wrong with you, and what doctor told you so?"

"Keep your voice down," Bill warned him. "You ain't an auctioneer. Look, kid, you yourself cross that office complex plenty after dark. You've already told me they only have one guard for the whole area after the day shift ends."

"Sure," Josh conceded. "Because all the big bosses are gone. But—"

"All right then. One guard, and I'll handle him."

"And what do I do?"

"You been to high school, and you ain't figured that out yet? I just got done telling you that Stratton has got a man going through Beckman's desk."

"So you want me to take something from Stratton's desk—"

"Just a copy that you're going to make right there."

"You want me to copy something," Josh resumed, "then put it in Beckman's desk?"

"Sure, that's the gait, kid. Easy as pie, ain't it? Something that Beckman has no damn business having, see? Something that might go bad against Stratton in a court of law."

"Like what?"

"I'm the muscle, Joshua, *you're* the brains in this outfit. You figure that out. I trust you. Just remember, the big idea here is to get me promoted into Beckman's job. That's the quickest way I'm going to find out exactly which men are part of the Regulators. The law needs specific names linked to specific crimes. John Doe warrants are worthless for serious prosecutions."

Actually, Bill's risky plan was a pretty good idea, Josh told himself.

Bill slyly added the clincher.

"And kid? When all this is over, just think what a story it'll make. What's that big scribbling award they give at Harvard?"

"The Golden Quill," Josh replied in reverent tones.

"There you go. Why, you win one of them? I'll bet that editor of yours will even raise your remittance payments."

"All right," Josh finally surrendered. "When?"

"Time is nipping at our sitters," Bill reminded him. "We better try this very night. Maybe around midnight."

Before either man could say anything else, a Chinese youth in a floppy blue blouse stopped at their table. They recognized him as one of the Number 10's full-time employees—one of the workers who helped drag Danny Stone's dead body outside.

The kid bowed politely and handed Hickok a folded note on perfumed stationery. Josh watched his mentor read it, then flash a curious little smile.

"Interesting," Hickok said, letting Josh read the brief missive. It was written in bold penmanship with plenty of royal flourishes.

Dear Mr. Lofley, Josh read, *if you glance at the far end of the bar, you will notice a blue chintz curtain. The stairway behind that curtain is private and leads to my suite upstairs. I know your lunch break is brief, but could you possibly find a few minutes for me? I have some information for you. Cassie Saint John.*

Bill crumpled the note and shoved it into his pocket. Later, Josh knew, he'd burn it. The youth was immediately worried. He had seen no sign of Cassie today—nor of Stratton, Morgan, and Beckman.

"It might be a trap," he warned Bill. "She lures you upstairs, and they kill you."

Bill mulled this and shook his head. "Why there? Why get blood and gore all over her place?"

"They don't need to shoot you," Josh reminded him. "Labun carries a nasty club on his belt. You yourself told me more men are bludgeoned to death out here than shot."

"You could be right," Bill was forced to concede. "You're learning how to think, Joshua. Hell, I'm s'posed to die in the Number 10, if you go by prophesy."

"Sure. And where's Deke? He's usually in for lunch by this time."

Hickok nodded patiently. "All true. But like I said, we can't afford to hedge. And it ain't just the big bosses I got to fret."

Wild Bill pointed his chin toward the bar. Calamity Jane—Jim Bob Lavoy to everyone else—had seen the Chinese worker deliver a note to Bill. And the stone-cold stare she gave him now made it amply clear Jane also knew who wrote that note.

"I might get shot in the ass for parting those curtains," Hickok mused. "Or shot in the pizzle when I sneak back down."

Bill glanced at Jane again, then at the perfumed note. He sighed.

"It's not just those big green eyes, Longfellow. Duty calls the Pinkerton man. She claims to have information."

"Yeah," Josh replied sarcastically. "Duty calls. But I've noticed that when you're involved, duty's call always sounds just like the Siren's song."

Hickok waited until Jane was making change at the cash drawer. Then he ducked past the curtains and opened an unlocked door. It gave entry to a narrow stairwell that smelled of beeswax polish.

A carpeted landing at the head of the stairs led to two doors, both of them marked PRIVATE. Wild Bill held his breath when he spotted an armed guard sitting on a wicker settee just past the top stair riser. One of the mining company guards,

Bill saw from his cheap badge. Compliments of Deke Stratton.

However, Stratton's man only gave him a knowing wink. "It's the door on the right," he told Bill, trying not to smirk.

The guard held a sawed-off shotgun in his lap like a favorite pet. Bill tried not to think about it, centered on his back, while he waited for Cassie to answer his knock.

"Mr. Lofley! How very kind of you to come!" the pretty blonde greeted him effusively. "Won't you please come in?"

Hickok couldn't help wondering if Josh wasn't right. His eyes rapidly shifted angles to check for danger when he stepped inside.

All he found, however, was a sumptuously appointed suite of rooms. Gold fleur-de-lis wallpaper and white ecru rugs made a sharp contrast with the rough saloon below.

Bill breathed deep of the room's feminine bouquet: jasmine and honeysuckle. He took in gilt chairs and a white brocade couch. Beautiful wash drawings were framed in gold scrollwork—scenes from Paris, Rome, Madrid, London.

Cassie saw her visitor admiring the drawings. Bill didn't bat an eye when she used his real name.

"I've visited all those places, Mr. Hickok. Even had lovers at some."

"I would hope so," Bill assured her. "Certainly in Paris."

She smiled. "I won't tell! But do you know? 'Memories' are highly overrated. Nothing but potpourri in a covered jar, really."

It was Bill's turn to smile. "Less tangible than that, even. It's experiences, sensations, we crave."

"Yes, exactly. So I mean to go back to all those places."

Bill gave a slight bow to acknowledge her wisdom. Cassie looked stunning in a pinch-waisted dress of emerald green.

"But that will require a lot of money, Mr. Hickok."

"Please . . . call me Bill, Miss Saint John."

"Only if you'll call me Cassie."

Bill spread his hands in the European gesture of surrender. "You drive a hard bargain. Cassie it is. About all this money you'll need, Cassie. I assume that your, ahh, association with Deke Stratton has not been detrimental to your savings?"

She had to smile at his diplomacy. "I'm grateful, Bill. I see you understand my situation well. Deke Stratton can easily trick the eye. But he's a callow man who fools the decent with good tailoring. He's also immensely wealthy."

"Mm . . . and getting much wealthier than most people know, I'd wager."

Cassie shrugged. Her hair was freshly washed and fell, unrestrained, to cover one side of her face.

"The money part is his business," she replied as she strolled toward a folding Japanese screen that stood between her and her visitor. "But I hope Deke and his cronies pay for the murders they've ordered or carried out. Not just Owen, but Butch Winkler and Esther Emmerick and all the rest of their victims."

By now Cassie was watching Bill over the top of the screen as she began undressing. "You won't mind if I change, will you? I go on duty soon."

"By all means," Bill invited. "Take off anything you feel must go. Tell me, Cassie . . . how badly do you want them to pay? Badly enough that you'd provide a sworn deposition against them?"

"A deposition, yes. I will not appear in court, however. Not against a man as powerful as Stratton."

Cassie's dress flopped over the top of the screen. Her big green eyes met his gaze frankly as she continued to strip.

"A deposition, ahh, is good enough," Hickok assured her, trying to concentrate on business. "Is that why you asked me to come up here? To let me know you want Deke and his pals to answer for murder?"

"That's one reason," she said, her voice teasing him as she draped her embroidered chemise over the screen. "I'll help if I can. Another reason is to warn you. Deke genuinely likes you—I think. But Beckman and Morgan both suspect you."

"Of being Bill Hickok?"

"That, my lands no! I don't think so. It would throw them into a panic. But they definitely don't trust you. They believe either that Mr. Pinkerton hired a gun tough or that someone else sent you."

Still holding his gunmetal gaze, Cassie draped a pair of frilly pantaloons over the screen.

Wild Bill swallowed with an audible effort. "I 'preciate the warning, Cassie."

"Well, there's more. Beckman's in a rage today.

Those six horses you shot—don't deny it, Wild Bill—well, the riders were some of Beckman's Regulators. Doing some 'night riding,' as Beckman calls it. They swear only a professional gun slick could have done it at such range."

Bill looked at all that clothing, still warm from Cassie's beautiful body. Involuntarily, he moved a few steps closer to the screen.

"By now," he said, "I'd guess you must be naked?"

Cassie flashed a mouthful of teeth like tiny polished pearls. "Bare-butt naked," she assured him. "Not a stitch on."

Bill took another step, his breathing quickening.

"Hold it right there, handsome," Cassie ordered in a no-nonsense voice.

Bill halted as ordered, but only reluctantly.

"First of all," she told him, "I'm supposed to meet Stratton downstairs in fifteen minutes. What's the point of starting something we couldn't finish—adequately, I mean?"

Bill grinned at her candor. "You can't rush a fine Chablis," he agreed.

"For another thing," she went on, "you've been listening to too much saloon gossip. All that scuttlebutt about how Deke Stratton plays me like a piano. You figure it'll be easy with a secondhand woman like me, don't you?"

"If you're secondhand, Cassie," Bill told her sincerely, "then new goods are worthless."

He bowed again and headed for the door. But evidently he had found the right gallant answer.

As he grabbed hold of the fancy glass doorknob, Cassie called out his name.

"Wild Bill?"

When he turned around, he saw the beauty had stepped from behind the screen. Bill forgot to breathe as he took in her sleek ivory nakedness: the firm, heavy, high breasts, flat stomach, and flaring hips.

"Forget that second reason," she assured him. "It's just that we don't have enough time for fine wine . . . right now."

The dormitory provided for bachelor clerks and copiers was basic and Spartan, like an army barracks. Each man was provided a narrow iron bedstead and a thin cotton pad for a mattress, with one shoddy blanket apiece. A wooden footlocker held each man's personal gear.

Shortly after sundown, when the workday ended, Josh ate a quick supper purchased from a vendor. Then he paid a Chinese water boy on the night shift a dime to come wake him up at 11:15 P.M.

Josh took a quick bath at the bathhouse next door operated night and day by Chinese workers—thousands of whom remained out West after the transnational railroad was completed. Then, as Hickok had ordered, he donned the darkest clothing he owned.

That illegal bar key Hickok had given him seemed to burn in Joshua's pocket, reminding him of its dangerous presence. Bill had agreed to meet Josh where the main footpath, which crossed the office complex, intersected with the gravel road used by the big ore wagons.

"Psst! Longfellow. Over there."

Josh saw Bill lurking in the shadows behind a big heap of old mine tailings. He had his scatter-gun with him.

"Stratton's office is deserted," Bill confirmed. "And just like you said, there's only one guard. I been watching his route, so I know when you'll have the most time. You'll do everything by my signals, got it?"

Josh was too nervous to trust his voice. So he only nodded.

"Move up the slope over there," Bill went on, pointing to a sprawl of tar-paper shacks and clap-board shebangs. "The guard don't walk through that part. Then cut behind that pile of timbers, see 'em?"

Josh nodded again.

"Just lay low until you hear me give the owl hoot. One long hoot means it's safe to unlock the door. I'll be right outside the whole time."

Josh finally found his voice. "What about light? It's pitch-dark inside."

"There's only one window, and it's got the shade down. Use this"—Bill handed him a stub of a can-dle and a few phosphors—"but keep it low, way down by the floor if you can. If I give two owl hoots, that means snuff your candle—guards coming. Got all that?"

"Yeah, I think so."

"Got you a pencil and paper?"

Josh patted his hip pocket. "Right here."

"All right, kid, you know what to do. Get something juicy and incriminating. Something Beckman has no business possessing. We play this thing right, and Ben Lofley will soon be head of security at Harney's Hellhole."

"Yeah, unless we're walking into a trap. What then?"

Even in the gathering darkness Josh saw Bill's teeth flash in a grin.

"In that case," Hickok replied, "I'll see you in hell, Joshua."

Chapter Eleven

When the guard was far off down the slope, Wild Bill took up a good position behind one corner of the plank building. Then he gave the owl hoot.

Right on cue, Joshua came scuttling out from behind the big pile of timbers. Even in the generous moonlight, he was hard to spot in his dark clothes. He paused a few yards from the building, screwing up his courage.

Hickok, who never did anything by halves, swore under his breath.

"This is no time to go puny," he warned Josh from the shadows. "There could be a roving sentry, too."

Bill held the pump-action scattergun by its pistol grip, hoping to God he didn't have to use it. The gun was effective and dependable, but also explosively loud—one shot and every Regulator in the area would be swarming on them.

Josh's hands were steady enough. But the damn bar key was clumsy and hard to figure out, at first.

"Any old day now, kid. The hell you doing, playing tiddlywinks?"

"I'm no criminal, how should I . . . I mean, not one of these stupid . . . *there!*"

The hinges made meowing noises when Josh finally nudged open the office door.

"Don't stand there gaping, you numbskull! Hustle your bacon inside and shut that damn door. Light kept low, you hear two hoots, douse your candle."

"Got it."

Josh eased himself around the door and closed it. With the window shades down, the interior was as dark as the inside of a boot. But he had seen where Stratton's huge desk was when the door stood open.

Josh crossed to the desk, then knelt behind it and fished the candle and matches from his pocket. He scratched a phosphor on the unsanded floorboards, then lit the candle.

Ears straining to hear Wild Bill, Josh started rummaging through the drawers. The wide top drawer held nothing but steel nibs, bottles of ink, blotting paper, and the like. But the first side drawer he pulled out contained various files: IN-VOICES, ACCOUNTS PAYABLE, SUBCONTRACT JOBS.

One labeled simply LIBERTY caught Josh's eye. He pulled it out, put it on the floor in the circle of candlelight, and began examining the contents.

* * *

Bill knew the kid would require some time inside. He had to find a good document, then copy it. Actually taking it would be too blatant; besides, that wouldn't fit Beckman's modus. So Hickok settled in for a wait, staying as alert as a hound on point.

A faint scraping noise behind him, about ten minutes after Josh went inside, made Hickok spin around on his heels, scattergun at the ready. But it was only Joshua—he had reached around the window shade to unlock the window and crack it open a few inches.

"Bill!" His voice was excited.

"What the hell are you—"

"Bill, listen to this! I've found a file labeled 'Liberty.' It's full of credit vouchers for the Liberty Mining Company. It's from the smelter at Devil's Tower, Wyoming. Man alive! There's a total of $166,000 for four different loads of gold ore."

"Four?" Bill whispered back, forgetting his irritation at the kid. "That's how many wagons have supposedly been heisted. That's good, kid—copy it twice and keep one for us. Quick now!"

Bill could hear the guard trudging up the slope. He leaned toward the open window and gave two owl hoots. Joshua snuffed the candle until Bill sounded the all clear.

Hickok heard his companion return to the desk to finish his copying job. Bill moved back up to the front corner, peeking around it to check on the guard. He was a comfortable fifty yards away, sneaking a smoke behind a shaft house.

More time ticked by uneventfully. Only later,

when it was too late to matter, did Hickok realize his mistake.

At that moment a long, five-second shrill of the giant steam whistle announced first break for the night shift. That also meant five seconds when Bill couldn't hear anyone approaching. So he should have turned around to look behind him.

Too late, he felt cold steel kiss the back of his neck.

"Don't get spooky on me, mister, whoever you are," ordered Merrill Labun's voice. "One quick move, and I'll let moonlight through you."

Aww man, Josh thought as he faithfully copied the dates and figures by candlelight. If this is what he and Bill thought it was, Deke Stratton's cake was dough! Unless everyone at Devil's Tower was on Deke's payroll, these ore shipments could easily be verified.

He finished his two copies and returned the original document to its manila folder, the folder to its drawer. Josh tucked the copies safely into his shirt, then snuffed the candle, preparing to leave.

A breeze nudged the window shade into rattling motion, startling Josh.

Cripes, he thought. I forgot to shut and lock the window.

He was about to thrust his hands past the shade when Josh started, hearing a familiar voice outside.

"Now turn around slow, mister, real gradual like. I wanna know who I'm killing."

For a moment, panic iced Josh's veins. But some part of him realized he must act now or all hope was lost.

With one hand, Josh clawed the parchment-textured shade aside; with the other, he dug the pinfire revolver from its shoulder holster.

He had no time for finesse. Josh spotted Labun's shadowy mass, right behind Bill, the big 44.40 pistol even bigger in that moonlight. The window shattered like skim ice when Josh rammed the pinfire's muzzle into it. The small-caliber French weapon used a small powder load and was not loud. But Labun gave a satisfying grunt of pain and folded to the ground, clawing at his wounded side.

Bill scooped up his weapon and tore around the corner just as Joshua flew out the office door, not bothering to lock it—what did it matter now? Labun began yelling "Code One!" over and over—obviously the signal for a major security breech.

"Good work, Joshua," Bill told the reporter. "You saved my bacon that time, scribbler. You get the copies?"

"Both of 'em."

"Good man. Now we got to get one of 'em in Beckman's desk quick while everybody mills around Stratton's office."

"Damn it, boss, I didn't *see* the son of a bitch's face," Labun insisted yet again. "I was just about to when his partner inside plugged me. *Ouch,* you damned mule healer, that hurts. Damn you to hell!"

"You need more whiskey," snapped the camp doctor, a former Army contract surgeon who had been dismissed for severe drinking problems.

"*You* don't need no more, you butchering bastard. *Oww*, damn you!"

"Take the pain," Deke Stratton snapped irritably. He was crowded into the doctor's tiny office at the rear of the general store run by the company. Deke had been able to respond quickly because he had stayed late at Cassie's, in town.

"You ain't the one gettin' a slug cut outta your ribs," Labun reminded him.

"You'll live," Stratton assured him. The manager of Harney's Hellhole paced the small room. He was too nervous to mind the stink of ether and carbolic acid.

Stratton watched what he said in front of the doctor. But he had to find out who was in his office tonight and what was taken—or more likely copied. He had a hunch that Earl Beckman's toady—whoever he was—had almost been caught red-handed. Deke made up his mind on the spot.

Since Merrill obviously couldn't search Earl Beckman's desk tonight, Deke himself would.

Two days after the incident at Stratton's office, a sea change took place in the social order at the Hellhole.

The day began with Earl Beckman's tragic and fatal accident. According to witnesses, the security chief somehow stumbled under a huge steam shovel and was instantly crushed to death. By noon flags all over the work site flew at half mast.

As for Joshua—he goggled as openly as Calamity Jane did when Hickok entered the Number 10 for lunch. Josh instantly understood he would not be having his meal with Wild Bill—Hickok was wearing the solid-gold badge of the Security Chief. And he was flanked by Keith "Boomer" Morgan and Deke Stratton!

As usual, Cassie Saint John left the faro table to join them. Josh, unlike Jane, felt immediate elation. Bill's ruse had worked after all.

Josh squeezed into an empty seat at a table occupied by his fellow clerks. A few nodded to him, but most were busy wolfing down their meal—half the noon break was wasted walking into town and back.

As Josh forked hot meat pie into his mouth, he wondered what Deke and Bill were so engrossed in talking about. It made Josh recall those credit vouchers: $166,000. The figure was almost incomprehensible to him. Josh lived on a newspaperman's annual salary of $350.

Thus ruminating, Josh almost choked when Calamity Jane—Jim Bob to the rest of the world—jabbed a sharp elbow into his ribs.

"Meet me out at the jakes," she said low in his ear.

Reluctantly, Josh waited a few moments until she was out of sight. Then he went out back where a straddle trench had been dug so customers could relieve themselves.

Whatever Josh had been expecting, Jane's question took him aback.

"How bad are Bill's eyes, Joshua? Straight-arrow now!"

"You noticed too, huh?"

Jane gave him a look like he was pitiful.

"Sorry," the reporter said sheepishly. "I forgot I'm talking to the best female shooter in America."

"Wall, this little Annie Oakley is the best. But I'm damn good, tadpole. Tell me about Bill's eyes."

"He's still sharp up to the middle distance," Josh replied. "And he can still plug big targets like a horse at long range."

"He's still good for a showdown then," Jane said, somewhat relieved. "But he's more vulnerable to dry-gulchers in the dark or at long rifle range."

Josh nodded. "That's how I see it too."

"That man is too damn vain to ever wear specs," Jane mused. "I know him. He'd rather die purdy and blind. Figures 'em big-boobed blondes like Cassie won't cotton to him then. Well, he's in the goddamndest fool mess now, and *both* of us better cover his ampersand."

A group of miners came out back, unbuttoning their blue jeans, and Josh and Calamity Jane returned to the Number 10. Joshua was cleaning his plate with a heel of bread when Cassie got up to return to the faro game.

She brushed close behind him, so close Josh smelled her hyacinth perfume. While all the clerks were drinking in her face and bosom, Cassie dropped a little slip of paper beside Josh's plate. He covered it with his hand and didn't read it until he was alone outside.

It was a two-line note in Bill's plain handwriting:

Rent a rig tonight at the livery. Wait for me there.

"Well, Earl's gone now," Deke said after Cassie had left the table. "Hell of a thing, poor guy. It was a hard death, but mercifully quick, I'm told. I propose a toast: To our new security chief, Ben Lofley."

He, Wild Bill, and Morgan all clinked glasses, then took sweeping-deep swallows of the cold lager.

"You'll soon have the hang of Earl's job, Ben," Deke assured him. "The main thing for you to plan right now is that little matter we spoke of earlier at my office."

"The problem with the Sioux, you mean?"

Stratton nodded, knuckling some foam off his neat black mustache. "The latest letters from our foreign partners have demanded some kind of . . . corrective action against that Copper Mountain bunch. That's understandable, of course, given these robberies of gold lately."

"Of course," Bill repeated, noting the ironic look exchanged between Deke and Morgan. Neither man had clearly admitted yet, to Bill, that they were stealing gold ore for themselves. But obviously they were letting him guess that for himself.

"This corrective action," Deke resumed, "should not wipe the savages out or anything that drastic. The Indian lovers in Congress would have a fit."

All three men laughed.

"Try to arrest their leader," Morgan chipped in. "This Wolf Boy or whoever."

"Coyote Boy," Deke corrected him.

"Right. Silly damned savage names."

"They can be funny," Deke pointed out. "I knew a Pawnee once who liked to drink whiskey with miners. His people took to calling him White Man Runs Him."

Bill grinned. "That's nothing. I knew a fat-ass Sioux called All Behind Him."

Again all three men laughed, as friendly as barracks mates. But Hickok was fooled by none of it. Hell, only hours earlier these "affable" men had murdered Earl Beckman.

Besides, there was still the problem of Merrill Labun. He shared a nearby table with several other security men. Though he still favored his wounded side, he was recovering fully from the wound.

In theory, Bill realized, Labun was his subordinate now. And so far he had played his part willingly—too willingly, it seemed to Bill. Deferential to the point of servility. But Hickok didn't trust it.

He recalled something Deke told him a few days ago: *I have Earl's desk searched.* Labun must be the secret dirt worker. He answered directly to Deke Stratton only—Bill was sure of that.

Finally Hickok was right where he wanted to be: At the center of the swindle at Harney's Hellhole. The big question now was, how the hell would he get out of it alive?

Chapter Twelve

"But *why'd* you have to trust Cassie with a note?" Josh argued as their rented buggy rolled out of Deadwood at a brisk clip.

"Simple," Bill assured him, shaking the reins to keep the gray gelding at a trot. "Because Deke Stratton trusts her, too. Thinks she's as loyal as a lapdog. It's one of his few blind spots—he underrates Cassie's independence.

"Maybe," Josh suggested, "you just *over*rate her loyalty to you."

"You writers created that monster, kid, not me. Used your slick way with words to build me up into a 'living legend.' Now, when I draw on that legend, you complain? I'd wager none of you will shed a tear when your damned 'gunfighter mystique' gets me shot in the back by trophy hunters."

Josh felt heat flood his face. Hickok's mildly

spoken indictment was "spot on," as Pinkerton liked to say. I'm the hypocrite here, Josh thought, not Bill.

However, Hickok allowed no man who sided him on the trail any luxury to fret for long.

"Even with the top up," he explained, "we ain't safe. I ain't had much time yet to study the work assignments Beckman gave his men. But I did see he's got two outriders posted from sunset to sunrise. All they do is scout the fringes of town. You watch the right side of the trail close."

Bill wore both Colts and his shell belt under an old hopsack work coat. The scattergun lay on the floorboards under both men's legs.

Josh followed orders and watched close. But Wild Bill's remark about Beckman's work assignments had intrigued the reporter.

"Do you know which men are actually the Regulators?"

"No list by that name," Bill admitted. "Here, take these."

Hickok handed the reins to Josh while he shucked the wrapper off a cheroot, then fought the wind for a light. When he had his cigar puffing just right, Bill took the reins back.

"No actual list," he repeated. "But there's about a dozen men, Labun included, who are on a list for 'special duty' pay. And maybe it's just coincidence, but several of the men, I've noticed, have heavy Southern accents."

"Coincidence my sweet aunt. It makes perfect sense. Beckman was a hold-out rebel, refused to surrender the Southern cause. So what makes more sense, to him, than to draw his Regulators from the ranks of Southern night riders? The same men who are trying to bring down Reconstruction and the Negroes."

"Now you're whistling, kid. That's 'bout how I see it, too. And that's why we've got to get word to Coyote Boy and his people. Pressure's on the bosses at Harney's Hellhole."

"Pressure? You mean it's time for them to put up or shut up, right? They've cried 'Indian' so long that now they have to take action against them?"

"The way you say, Longfellow. Their big idea is to arrest Coyote Boy and try him for theft and murder in the white man's court. Make an example of him to the others. Way I see it? They mean to stop their illegal operation now. Or maybe alter it. So this'll make it look like they caught their man."

"Man alive, Bill! That's got to be it! No Indian yet has ever been acquitted in a white court. They'll hang Coyote Boy."

"Naw," Bill said confidently. "Won't get that far. We're going to help Coyote Boy turn the tables on 'em."

Bill hushed the lad's eager questions by raising a hand. Hickok reined in the gray and they sat there in the silvery moonlight bathing the old stage road.

"Heard a puma," he finally said. "But it's just a kill cry, not a warning. *Gee* up!"

They rolled forward again as Josh began a rapid-fire string of questions.

"You know how I hate saying things twice," Bill

cut him off. "Just listen when I palaver with Coyote Boy, and you'll get all the answers you need. Right now, shut your gob and stay alert. It ain't just Regulators who might plug us—the Sioux keep night guards out, too."

Except when at war, most Plains Indians were notoriously late sleepers. Unlike white man's villages, where residents went to sleep soon after sunset, Indian summer camps stayed lively well into the night. Thus, many of the Copper Mountain Sioux were still awake when the camp dogs began a furious racket of barking and growling.

Bill fought to control the horse as the skinny, mean-tempered curs began nipping at its legs. He drove into camp slowly, aiming for the huge fire at the center of the camp clearing. He had to swerve around huge wooden racks set up for smoking fish.

"Coyote Boy!" Hickok called out as he wrapped the reins around the brake handle. "We come with open hands to share news with you."

The subchief stood out in his bone breastplate. He lowered his rifle when he recognized the visitors.

"Ice Shaman! Come and smoke the common pipe with us."

Bill sighed stoically. He knew the strict Indian custom when in camp, and Bill disliked the smoking ritual. Indians these days smoked foul tobacco, having abandoned their own kinnikinnick.

So first all three men—Bill, Josh, and Coyote Boy—smoked to the four directions while discussing trivial matters. Josh did a good job of not choking on the strong Mexican tobacco; later, however, he would vomit on the trip back to town.

Only when Coyote Boy finally set the pipe down on the ground could Bill turn to urgent topics.

Quickly he explained that the miners were planning a raid on the camp. But the chief's angry face turned sly when he learned that Hickok himself was to lead the raid.

"When?" Coyote Boy demanded.

"Soon. When the Dog Star is bright in the north sky, bright as the Pole Star."

The Lakota leader nodded, understanding the attack would come in about five sleeps.

"Since the murder of he who is gone," he said, avoiding McNulty's name after dark because a spirit might answer his name, "we have been punished by the Indian Bureau back East. No meat, no coffee, no new blankets for the short white days that will soon be upon us. Some of the younger bucks, as you can see, are preparing for war."

The visitors could indeed see signs of this. Most of the males in their fighting prime had cast off their white men's garments. Now they wore clouts, elkskin moccasins, and beaded leather shirts. A few of the warriors were busy making arrow shafts from dead pine and hardening the points in fire.

Bill spotted a few stolen Army mules with the U.S. brand on their hips.

"Those will be slaughtered and eaten," Coyote Boy explained, "to replace the beef and pork the hair-faces have taken from us."

"Only fair," Hickok conceded. "What *isn't* fair is the mismatch in weapons. The Regulators have repeating rifles. Your arrows are indeed deadly. But they are difficult to make, very time-consuming—look how few you have. What, perhaps five or six for each warrior? Coyote Boy, you know these white dogs will easily carry two hundred rounds each man."

Coyote Boy admitted this, listening intently.

"You have some rifles," Hickok went on, "but only a few. And like your German piece, most of them are old percussion weapons. Do you have powder and lead, bullet molds?"

Coyote Boy shook his head. "We try, but the treaty is strict and we are forced to trade with white-eyes thieves. The powder we do have is old and undependable."

"I figured as much," Hickok assured the warrior. "So I'm taking care of that problem. When the Regulators attack, your men will be able to match their firesticks with your own."

Josh listened intently while Bill explained his new plan. As security chief, he could come and go more freely. In the next couple of days, Bill would ride to the telegraph office at Lead. Pinkerton would be instructed to ship a crate of fifteen new Winchester '72s, as well as fifty .44 shells per rifle.

"Your typical whiteskin soldier," Bill remarked, "would scoff at going into battle with only fifty rounds. But a Lakota warrior is a bullet hoarder."

Coyote Boy grinned and nodded. "If possible, we will kill a few of these Regulators with rocks. They do not deserve bullets."

"One way or the other, they need killing," Bill agreed heartily. "Take their hair, too. That will unnerve the survivors, for these are cowards, not men. The ones who survive this raid will not be free long—I mean to lock them up."

They were ten minutes from the outskirts of Deadwood when a rifle blast spooked the gray. The slug ripped through the canvas top of the buggy, so close to Bill's ear he heard a hornet-buzzing sound.

"Halt!" a male voice commanded from less than twenty yards away. "Keep going and we'll kill your horse—for starters."

"Haw!" Bill sang out, drawing tight rein and engaging the wheel brake.

Tangled blackberry bushes and small willow trees crowded the road. They heard someone approaching from both sides. Two shadowy figures emerged into the road, rifles at the ready.

"Toss out your weapons," one of them commanded in a rough voice. "Try any parlor tricks, you'll be walking with your ancestors."

"I can't give you my gun, sir," Bill said in a mild, almost bookish voice. "But you're most welcome to a couple of the bullets."

Josh flinched hard when Hickok, gun hand hidden under his hopsack coat, fired just twice: One bullet for each man. Two clean head shots. Hickok swore by a brain shot, the only "guaranteed kill" with one bullet. Even a slug to the heart was not always fatal.

The buggy rocked as Bill hopped down and examined each man's face close in the cheese-colored moonlight.

"Both security men for the mine," he called up to Josh. "Though no badges on them now. Looks like I just killed Earl's outriders, kid. We best hightail it out of here."

"Deke won't like this," Josh fretted as Bill grabbed the whip from its socket and laid a few licks across the gelding's rump.

Josh's remark reminded Hickok of the three Pinkerton men murdered by these cutthroats. Bill had known two of them, even served in the war with one. All three left widows and orphans.

"Too damn bad what Stratton don't like," Bill replied. "He won't like it, but he'll have to eat it. And that murdering, thieving son of a bitch will eat plenty more before J. B. Hickok is done dishing it out."

"Boys," Deke Stratton said, "maybe we've all been too damn reckless lately, me more than anyone. I was slow to understand how fast things are changing out here. Hell, the West is closing down quick. The very progress that made us rich will now lock us up for our troubles."

Deke, Keith Morgan, and Merrill Labun shared Deke's office. He had called this emergency meeting—minus Ben Lofley at the other men's insistence. Deke wanted to discuss last night's killings of Pete Helzer and Dick Skeels out on the old stage road to Lead.

"Changing too fast," Stratton went on. Dark pouches of exhaustion smudged the skin under his eyes. The others had never heard him ramble on like this, and they didn't like it. "They're stringing this new devil wire all over the open ranges now."

"Boss," Labun said impatiently.

"And Christ, boys! Just last week, hanh? I read in *Leslie's Weekly* how this new Lightning Train just made it from New York City to San Francisco in three and a half days. Oh yes, we've all been too damned shortsighted."

"Deke," Morgan cut in sharply, "this ain't no time for philosophy. It wasn't us being 'reckless' that laid out Petey and Dick. It was two clean shots to the head."

"Damn straight," Labun said. "And I'd sure's hell like to know where Ben Lofley was when them slugs was fired."

"Always harping on Lofley," Deke snapped. "What proof have you got against him?"

"What proof have you got *for* him?" Keith answered in Labun's place.

"One thing against him," Labun suggested, "is how he seems pretty tight with that new clerk, Charlie Mumford."

"That's right," Morgan took it up, nodding his big, balding head. "Didn't those two hire on at the same time?"

"How would I know?" Deke snapped. "More or less the same time, I'd guess."

"What I still don't get," Labun complained, "is why Lofley got the security chief's job 'steada me? He's prac'ly a stranger."

Deke sighed deeply, then closed his eyes to massage the eyeballs with his thumbs.

"Merrill," he said quietly, "we've gone round and round on this before. You've got a more important job as *my* personal security man. I need you poking around behind the scenes."

"Well sure, but I could do both them jobs," Labun protested.

"As I recall," Deke pointed out, losing patience now, "Brennan O'Riley whipped your butt last year. And Lofley whipped *his*. Now shut your damn mouth, you whining female. We've got bigger fish to fry."

Deke scooted his chair back and stood up, pacing in front of the huge map behind his desk. "Lofley will lead the raid on the Sioux in just a few days. He has orders to arrest—or at least kill—Coyote Boy. Technically, of course, the raid's illegal. Only federals can mount force against a reservation. But with no lawman there to witness it, there'll be no charges."

"But ain't this a stupid move?" Labun demanded. "Who do we blame the next heist on?"

"We don't blame it on anyone," Deke explained. "Because there won't *be* another heist. If and when the plan starts up again, we modify the scam somehow. Leave the Indians out of it."

Labun, still pouting, said nothing. But Keith Morgan approved Stratton's words with a hearty nod.

"Deke's making horse sense now," he said. "We can still get rich, but we'll have to be more . . . whatchacallit, discreet. What's worrying me still is all this wondering if maybe we're too late? Pinkerton gave an interview to the newspapers. He swears to prosecute whoever killed his men."

"Yes," Deke said quietly, "I saw that, too. At any rate, the killer he means would be Merrill here."

Labun flushed beet red. "Yeah, and who gave the order?"

Deke ended the confrontation with a careless wave.

"Never mind," he told both men, nodding toward the map. It showed every shaft, tunnel, and stope in Harney's Hellhole.

"As our last resort," Deke reminded the others, "we've still got the Inner Sanctum. An entire stope, the size of a big ballroom, that everyone believes to be permanently closed off. Remember, boys, it's well stocked for any emergency. We can hide there up to thirty days, even more, then just sneak off at will."

Deke turned from the map to look at Morgan. "Keith? How long would it take you to activate those charges? They're all in place now."

The mine captain heaved himself out of his chair and moved close to the map.

"Hell, I can have galvanic plungers hooked up in about twenty minutes," he boasted. "The nitro charges are planted here at the bottom of the lift shaft; here in the middle of the first tunnel; and here in the chamber itself. Only the escape shaft isn't mined."

"How much control do we have over the charges?"

"They're set up with a series lead," Morgan

replied. "They can be detonated behind us, one by one, as we escape. Or the whole kaboodle at once."

"Yeah, well, all that's just peachy," Labun cut in. "If we live long enough to get down there. I still think you made a mistake, boss, in killing Earl to trust Ben Lofley."

"Maybe so," Deke admitted calmly. "If so, the mistake can be corrected. The first solid sign I see that Lofley is a plant, I'll kill him myself."

Chapter Thirteen

Merrill Labun spurred his horse up beside Wild Bill's.

"Be a good idea to send out flankers, wouldn't it?" Labun suggested. "Copper Mountain's only a few miles farther now. If they've found out we're coming, could be they'll attack our flanks."

"Usually flankers are good battle strategy at night," Bill conceded. "If it was going to be a real fight, I mean, against white men trained in battle tactics."

"I take your drift. Hell, you're right, chief. This'll be more like shootin' fish in a barrel than riding into battle."

Labun dropped back into formation. Replacements had quickly been named for the two outriders killed recently. Twelve men, counting Labun, formed a column of files behind their leader. They wore dark clothing and most had tied bandannas across their faces. Their rifles were already out of the saddle boots, butt plates resting on each man's thigh.

Bill knew he dare not ride his strawberry roan. That horse had been with him for two years now, and had become part of the Wild Bill sensation created by Josh and other writers. Hickok was already in danger of being recognized. Since Joshua obviously couldn't come along this time, Bill had volunteered his lineback dun for the campaign.

By now, Hickok hoped, the Sioux should be ready to host a lively reception. Bill had sent Josh to Lead last Saturday afternoon to pick up the rifles and ammo. The kid had delivered the crates on his way back to Deadwood.

Bill also hoped that, by now, every warrior had fired a few rounds in his new Winchester repeater, both to set battle sights and learn the workings of the superb Winchester '72—a weapon Bill rated right up there with a Studebaker wagon when it came to superior workmanship.

If his plan went well, this should be a night to remember for any Regulators who survived it. And since all of them were either murderers or accomplices to murder, Bill felt no regret for his part in it.

At the last timbered ridge overlooking the reservation, Bill stopped the men by raising his scattergun high in the moonlit night sky.

"Prepare for final movement to contact," he ordered with strict military formality. "Check your weapons, your ammo, then your horses. Knock any sand out of your bullets now, or you'll risk a stoppage under fire. Next check your horses. Look at the girth, the latigos, the stirrups. Also check each hoof for loose shoes."

"Sounds like you've done this plenty before," Labun said with genuine respect. Lofley's soldierly bearing, along with his evident eagerness to kill for the company, had begun to change Merrill's mind about him.

"Oh, I've sent a few featherheads to the happy hunting grounds in my time," Bill said modestly. "Nothing personal. I shoot what I'm paid to shoot, then walk away like it's none of my business—because it ain't."

"Holy Christ," Labun said softly, impressed but also a bit daunted by this man's coldness.

Bill kept his voice lowered. "All right, let's raise dust. We'll stage for the attack in that plum thicket out ahead about three hundred yards. That'll put us downwind of their mangy curs. From here hold your mounts to a walk or the bit rings will clink."

Labun was thoroughly impressed by now. "You're some pumpkins as a battle leader, Ben. I see Deke's instincts was good. Hell, you've got this fight figured down to the last detail."

Wild Bill had to make a real effort not to laugh outright. All these plans had in fact been hatched by him and Coyote Boy. Hickók only hoped the hotheaded Lakota warriors remembered not to shoot at the lead rider.

He stepped up and over, then settled his hips into the saddle.

"Ahh . . . who's leading the charge?" Merrill asked.

Labun knew the rules in combat: the second-in-command always led the actual fighting so the commander survived to fight on. But he was in for a pleasant surprise.

"The men who get the big money take the biggest risks," Bill replied. "I lead the assault; you ride behind me to relay commands back. We'll attack in a staggered-echelon formation. Keep the men at five-yard intervals. Never mind women and kids or the old ones, they're a waste of time and ammo. It's the armed braves we have to put out of the fight."

By this time Wild Bill was almost confident that few, if any, of his men would later blame his military knowledge or tactics for what was about to happen. Except for Labun, who would be closer.

They reached the plum thicket overlooking the Sioux camp in its hollow a hundred yards below them. Fires sawed in the wind, and a crowd had gathered to watch two adolescent boys locked in a wrestling contest.

Bill posted in the middle of the rank so all his men could hear him. He swiped at the gnats swarming his face.

"When I charge, that's your command to attack. Remember—this is a sweep, not a sustained engagement. We ride through once, airing as many fighting Indians as we can. We nab the big chief or, failing that, at least kill him. Then we regroup past those bluffs to the north. Make your final preparations, men."

Now all the horses stood prancing, eager for action. When the last man was ready, Wild Bill heeled the lineback hard in the flanks. He shot out across the grassy clearing, and with a collective shout, the Regulators followed suit.

As previously arranged, Hickok very soon fired both barrels of his Spencer shotgun, letting Coyote Boy and the rest know where he was in this melee. The Sioux had set up two defensive lines of riflemen hidden in shallow pits. They rose up now, yipping their fierce war cry.

A withering line of fire immediately stunned the attackers. Their brave battle cries turned into agonized death groans, or the surprised wails of the badly wounded.

"Christ!" Bill played his part to the hilt. "It's a trap, boys, belay the attack order! Sweep their far flanks to escape, then head for the rendezvous point!"

But even that apparently sound command was part of the trap. As the fleeing Regulators veered wide around the lines of rifles, they rode smack into the siege defenses. These included pitfall traps and trip holes that snapped horse's legs.

One scene took the breath even from a seasoned fighter like Hickok. He watched a desperate Regulator spur his horse hard to clear a line of bushes; an eyeblink later, the man flew over the pommel and broke his neck when he landed—behind him, his horse had impaled itself, midleap, on a line of pointed stakes. The death cry it unleashed drowned out every other noise . . . until the rider, still alive and shrieking, was scalped and castrated.

Wild Bill averted his face, tasting bile. A second later a stray bullet tagged his left calf, passing through clean and close to the surface. It was piddling, as battle wounds went, hardly even showing any blood. But he actually grinned at the burning pain—further proof he had not collaborated in this obvious disaster.

"Belay the attack!" Bill repeated to the thoroughly routed night riders. "Guide on me! This way, every man saves himself! Retreat!"

Next day, news of the failed attack at Copper Mountain swept through Deadwood like a comber.

One wounded man who had managed to escape bled to death during the ride back. He was hauled into town with his ankles tied under his horse's belly. In all, five men were killed, three wounded including Ben Lofley. Only four Regulators escaped unscathed—the first defeat in their long reign of terror.

On the second day after the ruinous attack, Deke Stratton again called an emergency meeting in his office. And once again Ben Lofley was deliberately excluded. This time, however, Stratton did not have to be convinced—thanks to startling new evidence, he finally realized who Ben Lofley really was.

"I still don't understand it," he told the men gathered round him in the rustic office. "You men who survived swear that Hickok fought well. Hell, he was even wounded."

"Prob'ly one of our own bullets," Labun insisted. "I been thinking on it. Lofley—I mean Hickok— fired his scattergun way before he had any target. I'm thinking it was a signal."

"Sure," piped up one of the Regulators. "Them Injins missed Hickok deliberate like. It was all planned out."

"I think I've already proved that," Keith Morgan interjected. "You've all got to see this."

Morgan rapped his knuckles on a buckram hardback titled *Heroes of the American Frontier*. It lay open to a page that showed an early sketch of Pony Express Riders Bill Cody and J. B. "Wild Bill" Hickok. The rare photo of Hickok showed him without his trademark mustache, sideburns, and long curls—almost a dead ringer for Ben Lofley.

"What first tipped his hand, Keith?" Deke asked.

"I started wondering, boss, when I noticed that 'Lofley' had him a gesture just like yours—he kept lifting one finger to smooth his lip, just like you do to your mustache. That made me think maybe this hombre had him a mustache for a long time. So I started leafing through all them books you've got out at the ranch but never read. Damn near crapped when I found this."

Deke nodded, his coffee-colored eyes thoughtful. The men surrounding him were Morgan, Labun, the teamster named Steve, and the Regulators who survived the debacle at Copper Mountain.

"Face it like men," Deke said quietly. "That bastard Hickok broke it off inside us. By now he's got more than enough rope to hang us all."

"Then why'n't we just kill him?" one of the Regulators demanded.

Deke snorted. Labun answered for him.

"*You* want to brace him, Johnny? A man who escaped from the Rebs three times, who took out the McCanles gang by hisself? A gunman with more than forty kills to his credit?"

The hothead flushed and fell silent.

All this prompted another man to ask nervously, "Where is Hickok now?"

"Relax. Today I sent him on a payroll run to Rapid City," Deke said. "He's not due back until tomorrow."

Deke, still calm and unruffled, next spoke in a tone of almost wistful regret.

"Boys, I never thought we'd crater first." He used a miner's term for caving in under pressure. "But we're whipped good now. Why fight a lost cause? Even if we could somehow plant Hickok, the damage is likely done by now. Pinkerton knows everything—names, dates, amounts, Christ knows what else."

"So what do we do now?" Johnny said. "Just hang up our shooters and wait for the big man to serve us warrants?"

Deke's eyes cut to the map on the wall behind his desk. He gave all of them a nervy little smile.

"Not at all. We've still got the Inner Sanctum, don't forget. A few weeks from now, everyone will think we're long gone—South America, maybe, or even Europe. The danger to us will go way down. Then we can slip up topside again, after dark, and really pull foot."

Deke's gaze swept every man. "It won't be ideal, but it will sure's hell beat a stone cell at Yuma. As of tonight, every damned one of us is going to literally disappear from the face of the earth."

With the illegal raid on a federal Indian reservation, Wild Bill finally had a specific crime and the specific names of perpetrators. Now he had only to wait for a special courier from Pinkerton to arrive with duly prepared arrest warrants. The most serious charges would fall to Stratton, Morgan, and Merrill Labun since Beckman was dead.

However, Wild Bill knew he had new troubles when, two days after the disastrous raid at Copper Mountain, Stratton sent him on a payroll run to Rapid City.

This was a task usually assigned to Merrill Labun. The only good reason for sending the security chief was to get him out of the way. So Hickok fully expected trouble when he returned from Rapid City.

What he did not expect, however, was to find all the major players gone. Vanished was a better word for it. Stratton, Morgan, Labun, even the Regulators who were still ambulatory—every one of them had evidently absconded en masse while Bill was gone.

Hickok immediately telegraphed Pinkerton, who proceeded to alert federal and local law officers in the surrounding states. Railroad and stage-line officials were also notified. Almost certainly these fugitives from justice had split up. The telegraph made it virtually impossible that all of them could slip through the ever-tightening net.

And yet, apparently, that's just what had happened. Later, on the first day of his return to Deadwood, Bill talked to Lonnie at the feed stable.

"None of them men left town that I seen, Ben," the kid insisted. He rolled his head over his shoulder to indicate the stalls.

"Mr. Morgan and some of them others? They've still got horses and saddles here. They ain't gone nowhere."

"No," Bill replied thoughtfully. "I reckon not."

But obviously they *were* gone. For one thing, Stratton had hastily appointed one of the subsurface-water engineers as temporary mine supervisor. Also, Bill found out a day later that Deke had deeded his horse ranch over to his foreman.

"It's just a paper arrangement," Hickok assured Josh. "It was done to thwart any grab by the law or angry creditors."

Josh had quit his cover job to work full time helping Bill with this baffling new twist. Hickok, however, still feared this town the way the Greeks feared Troy. So he still took pains to disguise his identity. Also, he hung on to his status as security chief—this left him free to poke around at will.

His efforts soon turned up an ominous bit of information: One of Keith "Boomer" Morgan's last official acts, before he disappeared with the rest, was to visit the powder magazine.

There, according to the requisition sheet he filled out as required, he checked out three galvanic plungers—electrical detonators for explosive charges—and an entire spool of copper electrical wire.

Bill mulled all those odd clues while he and Josh ate supper at a café across the street from the Number 10.

"Find anything in Deke's office?" Josh asked.

"If there was anything there, he took it," Bill replied.

"How about Cassie? She knows Stratton as well as anybody."

Bill grinned. "Better. That's why she's obviously keeping her mouth shut. She's sweet as clover honey until I mention the question of Stratton's whereabouts. Then, suddenly, she gives me the frosty mitt."

"She's protecting herself?"

Bill nodded. "Yup. Just like she expects Deke to look her up again. As if he's not very far away, even."

"Mr. Lofley?" a voice cut in. It was the young Chinese kid from the Number 10. "Miss Saint John sent this, sir."

The boy laid a folded note near Bill's plate and scuttled back across the busy street to the saloon.

"Perfumed," Josh said, feeling a sting of jealous envy as Bill unfolded and read the note. "Let me guess. She'd like you to stop by her suite later to look at her etchings?"

If Hickok heard his companion, his puzzled face

didn't show it. He stared at the brief message, frowning, yet excited too.

"Yeah," Bill muttered. "This is the key to the mint right here."

Josh pushed his plate away. "What?" he demanded. "What is it, Bill?"

"You're right, Joshua," Bill said thoughtfully. "Cassie does know Stratton well, and she is protecting herself. But she's also solid bedrock under those fancy feathers of hers. Look at this."

He handed Josh the note. There was no salutation or closing signature, just one puzzling line: *Fish go to the bottom in hot weather—or so I've heard.*

Josh shook his head. "I don't get it."

Bill flipped four bits onto the counter to cover their meal. "Good thing I do, ain't it? Let's get thrashing, kid."

"Where we going?"

By habit, Hickok carefully studied the street before he stepped outside.

"Fishing," he answered the confused reporter. "Hurry up while they're still biting."

Chapter Fourteen

"But you said you already went through Stratton's desk," Josh pointed out as Wild Bill led him into Deke's deserted office.

"Yeah. But now I need to look *behind* his desk," Bill replied as he crossed to the big map of Harney's Hellhole.

Bill began a close scrutiny of the detailed map. Josh, watching him, suddenly caught on.

"Man alive! Fish go to the bottom. I get it."

"What else," Bill assured him, "could explain the complete disappearance of so many men?"

"Aww man, what a story!"

"Yeah," Hickok agreed dryly, "when it's over. Which it ain't yet."

Josh, too, began studying the map.

"The stopes that're still active," Bill told him, "are numbered with an *A* after the number to

157

show it's still being worked. Ones with a *C* are supposedly closed."

"What does 'closed' mean? Just worked out?"

"And sealed. By law they have to blow up the tunnel leading in and seal off the access shafts from above."

"Cripes," Josh complained. "Look how many closed stopes there are. More than thirty. If Stratton and the rest are down there, they could be in any of those chambers."

Hickok nodded. Josh, eyes narrowed in puzzlement, watched Bill light a match and hold it close to the map.

"Why are you doing that?" Josh demanded. "Your eyes getting *that* bad?"

It was Josh's first mention to Bill of his failing vision. Bill heard him, but chose to ignore it.

"There," he said triumphantly. "Take a look. At closed stope number 13, see it?"

Josh moved closer and looked in the circle of light. Now he clearly made out a number of fingerprint smudges.

"All the rest are clean," Bill said. "But not this one. Stratton spent a lot of time looking at this map—looked at it most of the time he was talking to me."

"And he pointed to this stope more than once," Josh finished for him.

"Now you're thinking like a Pinkerton. C'mon, let's go take a look at the lift-shaft of 13-C, check out my hunch."

"Does it have to be number 13?" Josh complained.

"Of course it does," Bill said sarcastically. "This is Deadwood, ain't it?"

Stope 13-C was located far across the company lot, on a barren slope that had long been deserted. The shaft house on top, which once housed the steam lift to take workers in or out, had been leveled. That was true for all the abandoned stopes.

With one big difference here. When Josh and Bill, muscles straining, threw back the huge wooden cover, they did not find a shaft filled with gravel. The empty shaft gaped up at them like a hungry maw.

"You were right, Bill," Josh gloated, keeping his voice down.

"Something tells me," Bill said, "this is too simple. That *can't* be their only way in or out. They must have punched an escape shaft out, too. God knows where, though."

"What do we do?" Josh asked. "Get help and go in?"

Bill shook his head.

"It would take time to get enough men that we could trust. Besides, a posse of men would make so much racket going in, Deke and his bunch would have warning. Don't forget—Morgan took detonators with him."

Josh watched Bill shove his thin hopsack coat aside. He had donned his Colt Peacemakers since returning from Rapid City. Josh watched him palm both wheels, checking the action.

"We'll need rope," Bill said. "Plenty of it."

"We're going down there?" the kid demanded.

"I am. You're going to wait topside, in case they come up somewhere on the lot. Don't try to engage them if they do. Just fire your pistol into the shaft once as the signal I should come up."

"Bill, you've gone loco! I know you're some pumpkins with a gun. But there's nine, maybe ten of 'em down there!"

"I'm not going down there to kill them—this time," Bill assured him. "But first of all, we have to prove they *are* down there. And I've got to reconnoiter the situation. Until we know where those charges are and disarm them, nobody'll have a snowball's chance."

Hickok went to the tool crib and requisitioned several coils of brand-new hemp rope. But when they lowered it into the shaft, only about seventy feet were needed to reach bottom.

Bill secured one end of the rope through a knothole in the wooden cover with a strong double half-hitch knot.

"You stand on this to give it extra weight," Bill told him. "Plus you'll feel signals easy. When I reach bottom, I'll tug on the rope hard so you'll know. I shouldn't be too long. This trip is just a reconnoiter."

Josh wasn't too reassured. Bill had a way of deceiving himself with words—the look on his face said "showdown," to Josh.

Josh said, "What if . . . I mean, what do I do if you don't come up?"

Bill flashed his toothy grin. "You're a famous man of words, ain'tcha? Deliver a fine eulogy at my funeral."

*   *   *

The climb down was easier than Bill expected. But he quickly realized that was by design: the collaborators had dug plenty of footholds into the side. Bill was able to get down without keeping much of his weight on his arms. Unfortunately, very little overhead light penetrated to the bottom. Nor could Hickok risk bringing a light down here.

Bill gave the rope a few tugs so Josh would know he reached bottom. He scratched a phosphor to life and immediately spotted it: a nitro pack set to blow this shaft. Bill recognized the standard government-issue two-pound block of partially stabilized nitro in a yellow, waxlike base.

It was a mere few seconds' work to disarm the bomb by ripping the blasting cap and detonator wire off it. However, Bill knew volatile nitro still posed a danger—a sharp concussion, for example, could detonate it. So he took a few minutes to cover it good in a nest of rocks.

That explosive, Bill realized, had been wired in a series—other charges were also connected to this leadwire.

He listened for a long time, but heard nothing except his heart pounding in his ears. Wild Bill carefully groped his way down the dim shaft into the even darker main tunnel. The stope, he remembered from the map, lay about thirty yards dead ahead. A lit match now might easily be spotted. It was reasonable to expect guards at some point. So Bill inched his way forward in total darkness, hands following the detonation wire.

At one point, Bill thought he heard a scraping

noise somewhere behind him. He dropped, whirled, had a .44 leveled almost in a heartbeat. But he almost laughed out loud at the useless vigilance—Christ, he couldn't see two feet beyond his nose anyway!

Still, the feeling persisted that someone was on his back-trail. Only the sudden discovery of the second nitro pack took Bill's mind off the possibility he was being followed.

Good spot for the second explosion—must be about halfway to the stope, Bill figured. This could seal the tunnel and perhaps kill anyone in it.

Again, working in darkness black as new tar, Bill slid the blasting cap out of its well and tore loose the wire, disarming the bomb. This one, too, he secured in a solid nest of rocks.

Should be only one more, he told himself. And that will probably be in the stope itself.

All right, so why not retreat now? The kid was right—the odds were insane. And Hickok was definitely scared. Hell, the inside of his mouth felt like cotton. This, he realized now, was the true "hellhole" around here.

But stopping now felt wrong somehow in a way he couldn't shape with words. Like a wolverine unleashed, he wanted only to close for the kill. To the gambler in Hickok, it just made sense to keep going while he was on a roll. So he did.

By now his eyes had adjusted better to the inky depths. Though he could still make out little that was right around him, Bill now detected faint light ahead, coming, no doubt, from the open stope.

He continued carefully forward, both guns

drawn and cocked. Again, when he stopped to listen, Bill thought he heard breathing noises behind him.

"Joshua?" he asked the darkness in a whisper. But the empty silence mocked him.

Pulse throbbing in his ears, Bill resumed his forward motion. Gradually he drew closer to the illuminated stope. When still about ten yards from the opening, Bill finally spotted proof his guess was right: Deke Stratton, dressed in range clothes instead of his usual suit.

He was pacing back and forth in the middle of the lantern-lit stope. Bill saw what he was reading and realized they must be sending a man up into town. It was a copy of the *Rapid City Register*. Catching up on the latest news about his mystery disappearance, Bill surmised.

From this angle Bill could spot none of the others. But he heard their voices now and then. Deke was wearing a sidearm, and Bill assumed the rest were armed and ready, too.

I can't get the drop on all of them, Bill decided. Especially with no chance to spot my targets first.

He decided, with reluctance, to go back topside and figure his next play. But he also decided to move just a little farther forward to see if he could spot the final explosive charge.

Wild Bill's only mistake was underestimating Boomer Morgan's ingenuity. Bill didn't feel the very slight pressure of the tripwire until it was too late. With a popping *foosh* sound, the fulminate of mercury charge—the same type used by photographers for illumination—exploded, bathing the tunnel in intense white light.

Morgan had rigged the illumination charge to last longer than a photo flash. Its brilliant light revealed the lethal trap waiting for Bill: four men armed with rifles waited in the darkness, two on each side of the entrance to the stope.

In less time than a heartbeat, Bill saw it clear: even he could not plug all four. Not when they were ready and aiming at him. Then, in that same millisecond of wordless realization, Bill felt a shock of recognition. Calamity Jane stood on his left, siding him with her big Smith & Wesson already out.

She spat out the gunfighter's lingo curt and clear: "You plug noon to six, Bill!"

Hickok understood instantly that he was to kill the men on the right; Jane would target the left. The intense burst of gunfire made a hammering, echoing racket in that underground chamber. In two seconds it was history. All four men lay dead or dying, not one of them getting off a round in the face of these two superb shootists.

Moments after the four guards were killed, the fulminate burned out. Bill and Jane, blinded now, were left in the dark with their vision ruined.

They could only function in light. So Bill made a split-second decision and dove through the entrance of the stope. He tucked and rolled as a withering hail of gunfire greeted him. Merrill Labun and the remaining Regulators kept him pinned down while Deke and Keith Morgan ran toward a rope ladder on the far side.

Their escape hatch, Bill realized even as bullets whanged around his head. Jane dove in behind him and lay prone on the floor beside him.

"You fool, Bill!" she yelled at him even as she dropped a Regulator. "You're bound and goldang determined to die in Deadwood, ain'tcher?"

Bad as things were, they quickly turned desperate. Jane's six-shooter clicked, empty, and Bill was down to his last three rounds in one gun. He cast a desperate eye around the chamber and spotted it, right in the center: a canvas nitro pack.

"Pull back!" he shouted to Jane. "Fire in the hole!"

Bill scooted quickly back himself. But he stopped just past the opening. With rock dust flying in his eyes from enemy fire, Bill sent a quick snap-shot into the nitro pack.

He wasn't ready for it. The resulting explosion left his skull ringing for several minutes. Rock shards pelted him and Jane, opening tiny cuts all over their faces. But when the dust finally cleared, 13-C had finally become a "closed stope"—and a funeral vault for Stratton and his criminal cohorts.

"You okay, Jane?" Bill called out.

"Damn you, I'll live! But if you don't fight shy of Deadwood, Bill Hickok, it's going to kill *both* of us."

"Lady, I owe you," Hickok said, instantly regretting that he said it.

"You shorely do, good-lookin'," Jane agreed as she climbed out of the bomb rubble. "You shorely do."

* * *

Wild Bill Hickok took Jane's advice and got the hell out of Deadwood in a hurry. In fact, he and Joshua sneaked out of town that very night like two thieves in the dark.

But it wasn't bullets Bill most feared. Jane had gone on one of her wild benders, getting so drunk she shot out every window in town like a cowboy at end of drive. And once she had a skinful of rotgut whiskey, her horniness was legendary. So Hickok, the most feared man in America, lit out for Denver with his tail tucked between his legs.

At the end of their first day on the trail, the two companions made a meat camp beside the huge reservoir between Gilette and Sundance, Wyoming. The rugged Black Hills lay behind them now, dark humps on the fading horizon. Nothing but the wide-open expanse of Thunder Basin lay before them now.

"It's good you missed Jane," Josh commented as the two men cooked fresh trout in a firepit. "But too bad you missed Cassie."

Bill nodded, smiling in the fire-reddened shadows. The faro dealer had slipped out of town herself, realizing that Stratton's downfall changed things—her wagon was no longer hitched to a star. But Josh didn't realize she'd sent one final perfumed note to Bill:

Dear Mr. Hickok,
Obviously you won't be needing that deposition from me after all. I'm rich enough to go back overseas to live. But first I'd like to visit

*Denver for awhile. Look me up at the Crystal
Palace Hotel—if you're interested. We'll have
more than fifteen minutes next time. I promise.
CSJ*

"You think the Sioux at Copper Mountain will
be cleared now?" Josh asked.

Bill shrugged one shoulder. "Pinkerton knows
some of the head hounds in politics. I'd wager he
can at least get their full rations restored. I'm
guessing they'll come out all right this time. But
the red man's days are numbered, just like the buffalo's—one will go down with the other. And the
gunfighters with 'em," Bill added in a burst of candor that made him scowl.

"By now," Josh teased, "Jane must know you're
gone. She'll be hot on your trail before long."

Bill felt a shiver move down his spine. But he
also couldn't deny that, once again, she'd pulled
his bacon out of the fire.

"That woman's ugly as proud flesh," Bill said,
"and stinks like a bear's den. But I'm beholden to
her, kid, like it or no. I truly am."

"Yeah, well, I talked to your landlady Elsie,"
Josh said slyly. "She brought up her notion that
Wild Bill Hickok is secretly a gal-boy. Now, seems
to me Calamity Jane is a boy-gal. So maybe Jane's
right, after all?"

"Right about what?"

"Maybe you do complete her being?"

Bill's scowl etched itself deeper as he rolled into
his blankets. "Know what, kid? Your mouth runs
like a whippoorwill's ass. G'night, damn you."

Bill was tumbling over the threshold of sleep when Josh's voice jarred him awake.

"Bill?"

"What, damn it?"

"You may be scared stiff of Calamity Jane. But you're the bravest man I've ever known. It ain't just us writers, Wild Bill. You really *are* a legend."

Bill yawned and took one final look at the brilliant, star-spangled sky.

"I am, ain't I?" he said, accepting the flattery with no effort at all.

WILD BILL

DEAD MAN'S HAND

JUDD COLE

Marshal, gunfighter, stage driver, and scout, Wild Bill Hickok has a legend as big and untamed as the West itself. No man is as good with a gun as Wild Bill, and few men use one as often. From Abilene to Deadwood, his name is known by all—and feared by many. That's why he is hired by Allan Pinkerton's new detective agency to protect an eccentric inventor on a train ride through the worst badlands of the West. With hired thugs out to kill him and angry Sioux out for his scalp, Bill knows he has his work cut out for him. But even if he survives that, he has a still worse danger to face— a jealous Calamity Jane.

___4487-0 $3.99 US/$4.99 CAN

WILD BILL

JUDD COLE

THE KINKAID COUNTY WAR

Wild Bill Hickok is a legend in his own lifetime. Wherever he goes his reputation with a gun precedes him—along with an open bounty of $10,000 for his arrest. But Wild Bill is working for the law when he goes to Kinkaid County, Wyoming. Hundreds of prime longhorn cattle have been poisoned, and Bill is sent by the Pinkerton Agency to get to the bottom of it. He doesn't expect to land smack dab in the middle of an all-out range war, but that's exactly what happens. With the powerful Cattleman's Association on one side and land-grant settlers on the other, Wild Bill knows that before this is over he'll be testing his gun skills to the limit if he hopes to get out alive.

WILD BILL

JUDD COLE

SANTA FE DEATH TRAP

All Wild Bill Hickok wants as he sets out for Santa Fe is a place to lie low for a while, to get away from the fame and notoriety that follows him wherever he goes. But fame isn't the only thing that sticks to Wild Bill like glue. He made a lot of enemies over the years. And one of them, Frank Tutt, has waited a good long time to taste sweet revenge. He knows Wild Bill is on his way to Santa Fe and he is ready for him . . . ready and eager to make him pay. But after all these years he can wait a bit longer, long enough to play a little game with his legendary target. Oh, he will kill Wild Bill, all right—but first he wants Bill to know what it is like to live in Hell.

___4720-9 $3.99 US/$4.99 CAN

CHEYENNE

Spirit Path
Mankiller
Judd Cole

Spirit Path. The mighty Cheyenne trust their tribe's shaman to protect them against great sickness and bloody defeat. A rival accuses Touch the Sky of bad medicine, and if he can't prove the claim false, he'll come to a brutal end.

And in the same action-packed volume . . .

Mankiller. A fierce warrior, Touch the Sky can outfight, outwit, and outlast any enemy. Yet the fearsome Cherokee brave named Mankiller can snap a man's neck as easily as a reed, and he is determined to count coup on Touch the Sky.

___4445-5 $4.99 US/$5.99 CAN

Dorchester Publishing Co., Inc.
P.O. Box 6640
Wayne, PA 19087-8640

Please add $1.75 for shipping and handling for the first book and $.50 for each book thereafter. NY, NYC, and PA residents, please add appropriate sales tax. No cash, stamps, or C.O.D.s. All orders shipped within 6 weeks via postal service book rate. Canadian orders require $2.00 extra postage and must be paid in U.S. dollars through a U.S. banking facility.

Name_____
Address_____
City_____ State_____ Zip_____
I have enclosed $_____ in payment for the checked book(s).
Payment <u>must</u> accompany all orders. ❑ Please send a free catalog.
    CHECK OUT OUR WEBSITE! www.dorchesterpub.com